HER MARYLAND CRABBY DADDY

STATESIDE DOMS, BOOK 19

GOLDEN ANGEL

GTB PUBLISHING

Published by GTB Publishing

Cover art by Allycat's Creations

Don't miss a release! Sign up for our newsletter HERE!

*To the Facebook group Maryland is a Cult. Not a State:
We have the best flag.*

CHAPTER 1

<u>ETHAN</u>

"What do you mean your friend is coming to stay with me?"

This morning was not going his way already and his sister seemed determined to make it worse. She sighed heavily, as if he were the one being unreasonable. Thanks to video chat, he got to see the eye roll as well, and it made him clench his jaw.

He loved his sister, he really did, but it was a good thing she'd moved to New York a few years ago with their aunt and uncle or he might try to strangle her right now. On the other hand, if she hadn't been in New York, she wouldn't have met this friend that was apparently coming to invade his home. It had been nice and quiet since Molly moved north, and he liked it that way.

Now his peace was going to be broken by a stranger.

"I know it's kind of last minute—"

"Since she's coming today, it's more than kind of."

"But Ria needed to stay in Maryland for a bit, and I

have a room in Maryland that's sitting empty, so I told her she could use it."

Taking a deep breath in through his nose, Ethan closed his eyes and counted to ten.

"I know you're counting," Molly said.

And even though his eyes were closed, he knew that she was rolling hers again. She acted like *he* was the drama queen every time she did this. Not that she'd dropped an unwelcome, unexpected house guest in his lap before, but she had a habit of popping up with plans that she forgot to tell him about until the last minute. He hadn't known she was moving to New York until two days before it happened.

"Yes, I am, because I'm trying not to lose what little patience I have left," he said dryly. It wasn't just the short notice that got under his skin, it was the way she acted like it was no big deal. "How long is 'a bit'?"

"It's my house too."

Oh, that was not good. That was so not good.

"Technically it's not." But he knew that was hard for her to get through her head. Truthfully, it was hard for him too, although moving from his childhood bedroom into the Master had helped. Now his parents stayed in his old bedroom when they visited.

They'd retired and gone south, and he'd bought the house from them because he hadn't wanted to leave. He'd also done the brotherly thing and told Molly that her room was hers, at least until he got married and started a family, but that didn't look to be happening anytime soon. His last few dates had all been duds and his last serious relationship... well, it had been brought to his attention that he needed to work on being a better partner. Which had been lowering, but also made him wonder if he was even cut out for being in a relationship.

"It's my room." She jutted her chin out stubbornly. "You said it was. And I can do what I want with my room."

"Yes, but the rest of the house is mine. Is she just going to stay in your room and never leave? You don't think she might need to use the kitchen or the bathroom or something?" Yes, he was resorting to sarcasm, only because he already knew he'd lost this battle and he was annoyed about it.

It was pretty much a done deal, it sounded like. Molly had offered the room to this Ria, Ria had accepted, and she was arriving sometime today. There wasn't a whole lot he could do about it unless he wanted to bar Ria from entering the house, which would both hurt and tick off Molly.

But he still wanted to know how long he was supposed to put up with this person. The fact that Molly had diverted from, rather than answered the question, made him extremely suspicious that it was for more than a few days.

Today was Wednesday. Hopefully it wouldn't be more than a long weekend.

"You're going to be nice to her right?"

"How long do I have to be nice to her for?" he countered. Sure, he'd be nice. Civil, anyway. Nice might be beyond him, if he was being perfectly honest. His friends all called him their 'grandpa' friend even though they were all in their early thirties—according to them, he acted like a grandpa.

Though he hadn't actually ever yelled at kids to get off his lawn. He might have muttered a few things under his breath while his friends were over though, and apparently that had been enough.

"For as long as she's there," Molly said immediately. Yup, this was bad. Very, very bad. "She's a wonderful person, and she's very quiet and clean. You probably will barely even notice her."

"How long, Molly?" He gritted the words through his teeth.

She gave him a hard look through the screen.

"One month."

"One month?!"

"Ethan—"

"What the hell, Molly? A weekend is one thing, maybe even a week, but you expect me to live with a complete stranger for a fucking *month?*"

A squeaking noise behind him had him whirling around.

Ah, fuck.

A woman he'd never seen before was standing in the doorway between the hallway and the kitchen where he currently was. She was tall enough to come up to just under his chin, wearing a cute polka-dot pin-up dress that accentuated her curves—especially her cleavage—and her long brown hair was pulled back in a jaunty ponytail complete with a red bow that matched her dress. Her lips were also bright red, and her wide eyes were accentuated by eyeliner that came out in a perfect little wing that likely took a lot of practice to get right.

High-maintenance.

That was his first thought.

High-maintenance, but also hot.

"Sorry!" she said, backing away, pulling her rolling

suitcase with her. "Sorry... I just... I'll just go find a hotel..."

"Ethan!" Molly yelled at him through the phone. "Ria, don't you dare!"

<u>Ria</u>

Hitting the Maryland border had been exciting, mostly because she knew Maryland was a small state and once she hit the border she was almost there. Granted, she'd still had a little over an hour drive left, but that was 'almost.' She hadn't visited Maryland before. In fact, she'd barely been out of New York City, though she'd done some visits to surrounding areas.

Before today, the farthest she'd been away from home was Atlantic City for a friend's bachelorette party.

Well-traveled she was not.

But she wanted to break out of her shell and out of her usual space and... well, she also wanted to write about somewhere new. Daddy Doms in the big city did really well for her, writing under the pen name of Dakota Darling, but recently some of her fans had started asking if she'd ever write a book that wasn't set in New York City.

Which was when Molly had suggested visiting Maryland and getting a feel for it. Since she'd actually been reading some romantic suspense set in Annapolis, which sounded absolutely picturesque and like the exact opposite of the Big Apple, she'd decided to go for it. Plus, even though the trip was a research trip and technically a write-off, Molly had offered up her childhood bedroom in her brother's home as a place to stay, which would save Ria a lot of money.

It was supposed to, anyway.

Now she was backpedaling down the hallway, clutching her suitcase in one hand and the key Molly had given her in the other. She'd rung the doorbell and knocked, but apparently Molly's brother hadn't heard her.

He's a bit of a grump, but he warms up fast.

Molly's description had left out quite a bit of detail, including the fact that Ethan Davies was incredibly hot. Then again, being his sister, maybe Molly hadn't noticed. Ria hadn't been able to help but notice, considering that he was swaggering around in jeans that actually fit his very nice ass and a white tank top that showed off his upper-body muscles.

In fact, she'd been so distracted by his very nice ass that she hadn't realized what he was talking about until he'd started shouting at Molly about living with a stranger for a month. That's when she realized he was shouting about *her*. She was clearly unexpected... and he didn't want her here. Definitely not for a month. No matter what Molly had said.

"Wait!"

Ria glanced over her shoulder. Molly's brother was stuffing his phone into his back pocket and holding up his hands in a gesture of surrender. The expression on his face was no longer one of shocked anger, though he didn't exactly look friendly either.

"I'm sorry," she said immediately, guilt suffusing her. "Molly didn't tell me that she didn't tell you I was coming. I don't have to stay here."

"Yes, you do, or Molly will have my ass." As if to

accentuate his statement, his phone started buzzing, the vibrations loud enough that they could both hear it. He managed to give her a smile, but she could tell it was forced. It didn't reach his eyes. "Look, she surprised me, but that's not your fault. And you were expecting a place to stay, right?"

"I mean, yes, but it's not your fault and you shouldn't have to—"

"I don't *have* to. I *could* send you on your way but then I would have to put up with Molly for months, possibly years, afterwards. I'm sure we can manage to live together for a month, which will keep my sister from haranguing me for the rest of my life." He stepped forward holding out his hand. "Let's start over. I'm Ethan Davies, Molly's older brother."

It would be rude not to take it. Ria let out a slow breath and let go of her suitcase so she could.

"Rhiannon Sharp, though I go by Ria."

His palm was warm against hers, and a little frisson of awareness traveled up from her hand to her chest. She let go as quickly as she could without being rude. The last thing she needed was to be attracted to her best friend's grumpy older brother who didn't want her in his house. Yes, she'd immediately noticed he was attractive, but that didn't mean *she* had to be attracted to *him*.

"Nice to meet you," he said tightly, as though he was remembering exactly why it wasn't nice to meet her. Before she could tell him that she really was fine going to a hotel, he stepped around her and picked up her suitcase. "I'll show you to Molly's room."

She might have protested, but her phone started ringing. Reaching into her pocket, she pulled it out. Molly, of course. When she looked up, Ethan had already walked away down the hall and turned the corner.

Craptastic.

"Molly, hey," she said, answering the phone. She pinched the bridge of her nose and lowered her voice. "You didn't tell your brother I was coming?"

"Well, in my defense, I was in the middle of doing so and you got there a lot earlier than I thought you would. What time did you leave this morning? Two?"

"I kept waking up, so eventually I decided to just get an early start." Though now she was wishing she'd stayed in bed, even if it had meant staring up at the ceiling for another few hours. But she'd been so excited to get to Maryland and get started... Arriving early meant more time on day one to get a feel for everything.

Pressing her lips together, she wondered if she should go down the hallway. But she couldn't really stay here, could she?

"Don't let him drive you off, okay? I promise, he's a great guy, he just doesn't like surprises and, well, it's my fault. It'll just take him a bit to adjust, and I promise you, if he makes you go, he will never hear the end of it from me." The dire way she said it made Ria realize that Ethan had been right to worry about his sister's reaction.

Even though her instinct was to run, she didn't want to cause him more trouble than she already had. He told her to stay. And then carried off her suitcase, so it wasn't like she could just leave now anyway.

"If I leave, it will be because I wanted to, okay?" she said, squaring her shoulders and starting off down the hallway in the direction Ethna had gone. She was going to fix this somehow.

"Don't you dare. I know you, Ria. You'll leave even if

you have nowhere else to go just to make him more comfortable and I am not going to stand for it. I know exactly who to blame if you aren't staying there—and don't even think about lying, because Ethan will never go for that."

"What, because he always tells the truth?" No one always told the truth. Especially men, she'd found. Or, at least, the men she got involved with seemed to have a loose relationship with honesty.

Not that she was involved with Ethan Davies or wanted to be. No matter how attractive he was. So maybe the fact that she definitely didn't want to get involved with him was a sign that he was more honest than most of the men she'd interacted with in the past.

"Pretty much," Molly replied. Ria turned the corner and stopped short as Ethan exited a room at the end of the hall, no longer holding her suitcase. "It was really annoying when we were kids, but I got used to it. Anyway, you're staying. That's final."

"Is that Molly?" Ethan asked, coming closer. Ria's breath hitched a bit, her heart beating faster as he prowled towards her. The man really was far more attractive than he had any right to be.

"Yes. I'm trying to explain to her that it's not your fault if I stay somewhere else for the month."

"Don't worry about it, Moll. She's staying here, in your room. I just put her suitcase away." He glanced at her, studying her for a long moment, and Ria suddenly found it rather difficult to breathe under his intense gaze.

Crap, what was wrong with her? Just because he was hot didn't mean anything! Except it was something more than that, like some kind of magnetic pull that he exuded that made her breathlessly aware of him.

"I've gotta go to work. Just... stay quiet." With that, he moved past her.

Ria stepped back so he didn't touch her as he brushed by, finally able to breathe again now that his eyes were no longer on her. He went around the corner and she heard another door close.

"Where does he work?" she asked Molly, pressing the phone back against her ear.

"At home mostly," Molly admitted, sounding a little sheepish. "Look, I really am sorry. I didn't mean to make things more difficult for you, it was supposed to be the opposite. It really will be fine though, I promise. Just settle in and he'll get the stick out of his ass and you'll end up having a great time."

Right. Sure.

But she didn't know where else to go right now anyway and she didn't want Molly to be upset with her or Ethan, so it seemed like the best thing to do.

"Okay," she said, despite her reservations. "Thanks for letting me stay in your room." She mostly meant it.

"No problem. I'll talk to you later, okay? And just let me know if my brother starts being a dick. I'll get him sorted out."

Suddenly feeling very tired, Ria said goodbye to her bestie and headed into the room she'd be using for the next month. All she wanted to do was unpack and settle in. Hopefully everything would look better by the evening.

CHAPTER 2

The growling of her stomach woke Ria up, and she groaned, turning to her side and yawning as she stretched. The crinkling sound of her crinoline made her wince. She really hadn't meant to fall asleep. Heck, she hadn't thought she'd be able to, not after the way she hadn't been able to sleep last night.

Apparently getting up before dawn and driving for hours took more out of her than she'd realized. She kind of wished that would be something that could help her sleep in the future, but it wasn't the most convenient method of dealing with insomnia.

Pushing herself up to a sitting position, she yawned again and winced. Her poor dress was not meant to be slept in. Lifting her skirt, she made a face at the impressions the crinoline had left on her legs. That wasn't meant to be slept in either.

Her stomach rumbled again.

Food.

Food and then she'd figure out what she was doing for the rest of the day.

She still needed to finish up her work-in-progress, the final book in her current New York series, but she was also eager to get out and start exploring. Sure, it was a Wednesday afternoon, but that would probably be the best time to explore since it shouldn't be too busy. Annapolis was only about twenty minutes away. Maybe she could get lunch there. And then some groceries on the way back. Though she should probably see how much space there was in the fridge and the cabinets before she did that.

Hopefully Ethan wouldn't mind her carving out a little room for herself. She cringed at the idea of having to ask him for space.

Wandering back out to the main part of the house, she figured she could at least grab a glass of water before venturing into Annapolis to explore. Unfortunately, Ethan was in the kitchen again, standing at the counter making a sandwich. He looked up as she walked in.

No longer in the tank top, he was now wearing a dark-green button-down shirt that somehow looked even more attractive on him than when he'd been less covered up. Maybe it was the fact that he had the sleeves rolled up to the elbow, so she could really focus on his forearms and hands.

She had a thing for forearms and hands.

That tended to happen when a girl got into spanking books. Reading and writing them. A man rolls up his sleeves and, well...

"You hungry?" he asked.

Ria blinked. Oh. *Oh.* He thought she was staring at

the sandwich he was making. Thank goodness he had no idea the thoughts that had been running through her head.

"Do you like ham and cheese?"

"Um, well, yes, but…" Her voice trailed off as he took two more slices of bread out of the bag.

"Mustard? Mayo?"

"Just mayo please." Ria moved into the kitchen and sat on one of the stools across from him, watching him put together the sandwiches. This seemed like an olive branch moment and she didn't want to ruin it. "Thank you, I was hungry and planning on going out, but I don't know where to go yet. And I was also planning on running by the grocery store—could I pick anything up for you? Is there space for me to grab a few things? I know you weren't expecting me so it's fine if there's not, I'll figure it out."

Bemused eyes slowly rose to meet hers and he raised his brow at her, even as he continued to put together the sandwich without looking. Which was weirdly hot.

"Oh yeah? And if I said I had no room for your stuff, exactly how would you figure that out?"

Great, he couldn't just say yes or no, could he? Ria did her best not to scowl at him. She *was* the interloper in his house after all, and she wanted to be polite even if he wasn't. Though she would probably only be able to put up with that for so long. "I would ask you to make space, and go out to eat for a few meals," she replied primly. "If I needed to, I'd get a mini fridge to put in Molly's room for the time being."

"Well, you don't need to. There's plenty of space in the fridge and the pantry." He inclined his head towards a door on the side of the kitchen. "Just move some stuff around. Try to keep all your stuff in one place so we know what's yours and what's mine."

"Would you like me to label it too?" she asked, only a little sarcastically.

"That might help." If he heard the sarcasm in her voice, he didn't show any indication of it, slapping the top piece of bread on the sandwich and putting it on a plate to hand it to her over the countertop. "There's a few things we can probably share too. Milk, eggs, coffee, that kind of thing."

"Well, I prefer tea in the morning to coffee, but otherwise, that would be great. Speaking of, where are the glasses?" She started to get up, looking around. "I could use some water."

"Sit. I've got it."

The authority in his voice had her butt back in her seat before she could think. Ria blinked in surprise. That had never happened to her before.

She wanted to protest, but she was still in a bit of shock from both his bossy tone and her response to it. Bossiness was not usually her thing. In fact, the last time a boyfriend had tried to tell her what to do, it led to their breakup. Which *was* a little weird because she wrote about bossy Daddy Doms, but to be perfectly honest she'd kinda figured it was all fantasy.

That was how she'd gotten started after all, reading and fantasizing. But she'd never dated a guy who came anywhere close to fulfilling any of those fantasies, and normally when one tried to get bossy with her, her instinct was to fight back.

Yet here she was, butt in seat, while Ethan got her a glass of water.

Maybe because it was his house. She was used to letting someone else be the host in their own house, and yes, she was living here too but it wasn't like she was settled in yet. It didn't feel like her place or even a place she was staying, though she knew it would after a few days.

But she hadn't even slept one night here yet, so it still registered in her brain as Ethan's house, not hers. Especially since she didn't know where the glasses were anyway.

That must be it.

Ethan

Adorably rumpled. That was how he would describe Ria's current state of being. He wondered if she knew she had a crease in her cheek. Clearly, she'd taken a midmorning nap, which if she drove all the way from New York in the wee hours, made sense.

Still, he wondered what she did for a living that she could drive down on a Wednesday morning and then take a nap. Molly had said Ria needed to come to Maryland for research, but she hadn't specified exactly what kind or why.

Sliding the glass of water in front of her, he did his best not to think about how damn cute she looked like this, rumpled and not quite awake, mindlessly obeying his commands. Despite the way she sat back down when he'd ordered her to, he wasn't going to make any assumptions about her being submissive, much less the kind of submissive he needed.

"So, we should probably lay down some ground

rules," he said. "I don't know if Molly told you, but I work from home during the day, so I need it quiet. If you plan on staying out late, please let me know. It's okay to watch tv after I go to bed as long as it's not too loud."

He hadn't gotten a ton of work done this morning because he'd been too busy thinking about all the things he needed to tell her. All the things that Molly just automatically knew to do, but a stranger wouldn't, that he would require if she was going to be staying for a whole month.

"Anything else?"

There was a slight edge to her voice. Despite the way she'd sat for him, this was not a woman who was used to being told what to do. For some reason, her reaction just made him want to push her buttons more. Probably because he was feeling like his space and peace had been invaded.

"Yeah, the towels are in the linen closet next to the bathroom. Try to take your showers early in the morning or later in the evening."

She blinked at him. "You're seriously putting down rules about what time I come home and when I can take a shower?"

"Yes. I'm a very light sleeper and I can't sleep at all when I'm expecting someone back in the house, but I don't know what time they're coming in. I'd appreciate not lying awake waiting for you, wondering what time you'll be home. If you let me know what time, I'll at least be able to fall asleep for a while." This was something he'd learned with Molly. When his parents lived here, he'd been able to sleep through her shenanigans. Once they moved out and it was just him and his sister, for some reason it had triggered something in his anxiety, and he could only sleep if he knew where she was and when to expect her home. Ria might not be his sister, but he'd rather get the rules down now because he had a feeling he was going to feel responsible for her, as his guest. "And, like I said, I work from home. A lot of the time I'm on calls during the day, and the bathroom is right next to my office, and some of the pipes are creaky. And loud. Though, if you really need to shower in the middle of the day, you can just check in with me about when I'm on a call."

He pushed the thought of her showering in the middle of the day out of his head. He probably shouldn't have made that offer, because even if he wasn't on a call, knowing that she was naked and wet in the next room was hardly going to be conducive to working.

Taking a bite of his sandwich to give her a moment to think, he shifted, ignoring the way his dick had perked up at all this shower talk. Yes, she was very attractive. Yes, he was attracted to her. But he sure as hell wasn't going to do anything about it.

He'd already learned his lesson about fucking too close to home. Having sex with his little sister's best friend while she was living with him for a month would be an even bigger recipe for disaster than dating a friend had been.

"Right. I guess that's reasonable." She picked up her own sandwich to start eating.

Silence reigned for several long minutes. Ethan couldn't help but study her as they ate, trying to figure out what she was like. His sister was so extroverted and boisterous, he'd expected Ria to be the same—especially with the bright dress she was wearing—but unlike Molly she seemed unbothered by the quiet.

"So," he said finally, "Molly said you're doing research here? What kind?"

"Oh um, well, did she tell you I'm an author?" When Ethan shook his head, she blushed, which was odd. "Right well, I am, and I want to set my next series in Maryland, but I don't like to write about places I don't know. All my previous books were set in New York City and I want to do something different. I've read some books set in Annapolis, and when Molly said she grew up there and I could stay in her old room for a bit... well, it was too good an opportunity to pass up."

"Well, it's definitely different." Ethan smirked. "It's not a landfill after all, and it's not really a city. Not the way New York is."

Ria bristled rather than laughing, which had been his goal. "What do you mean it's not a landfill? Neither is New York."

"Not anymore, but it was built on one." He eyed her. "Did you really not know? A big chunk of the Big Apple is literally built on trash."

"I..." She glared at him. "You're making that up."

"I am not."

"I've lived there my whole life; I think I would know if it was built on trash."

"Apparently not." He smirked. The fact that he'd gotten under her skin made him feel a little better about having his house invaded. It wasn't very gentlemanly, but it was true. "Anyway, I've gotta get back to work. Feel free to look it up, I won't even make you admit you were wrong later."

He didn't really have to get back to work yet, he could have stayed to chat a little longer, but she was looking ticked off, so it was better to make a timely exit. Something else growing up with his sister had done for him: he knew when to retreat. Picking up his plate with his half-eaten sandwich, he headed back to his office, feeling strangely cheerful.

Maybe he'd use the time to look up Rhiannon Sharp and find out what books she'd written.

CHAPTER 3

What a dick!

The worst part was, he was right.

How come no one had ever told her that parts of New York City had been built on a landfill? And that parts of it were slowly sinking? Of course, there was that one section that was slowly rising.

Should she be worried about the kind of stress that would put on the skyscrapers? Were they all sinking at *exactly* the same rate or were some of them going to end up like the Tower of Pisa?

If there were structural issues, we would know.

Probably.

Ack. Great. Now she was going to be paranoid.

She needed to get out of this house.

Tiptoeing back to Molly's room, so as not to disturb Dickhead, she fixed up her hair in the mirror over the dresser and smoothed out her skirt. She hesitated, wondering if she should unpack or not, but considering she had nowhere to go this evening, it was probably better to leave that for now. That way if Ethan was still getting under her skin tonight, she'd have an excuse to sequester herself in Molly's room.

Besides, she wanted to go explore. She grabbed her laptop bag too. Maybe she'd find a coffee shop or something where she could get some writing done. Tiptoeing back down the hall, Ria paused in the front entryway to look up Annapolis and figure out exactly where she wanted to go.

It seemed like there was a lot centered around the harbor, so that's where she'd start. Plus, the online pictures were super cute. She had a feeling she'd set quite a few scenes there, so it would be good to get an idea of what it looked like in person. And there were plenty of restaurants, bars, and cafés where she could probably hang out. Hopefully.

Time to find out, anyway.

Hopping back in her car, she grinned as she headed out. Now she was feeling rested, fed, *and* she was excited to check out something new. It didn't take her long to find the aptly named Main Street and a spot in one of the garages. Despite it being a Wednesday in the early afternoon, there were plenty of people out and about, many of them looking like they were coming from lunch.

Main street was all shops and restaurants, and Ria paused to look at the menus as she walked down toward the water. It was a beautiful spring day, ten degrees warmer than it had been in New York yesterday, and she was eating up the sunshine and warm breeze.

"Love your aesthetic!" said a young woman with pink and blue hair as Ria walked by.

"Thanks! I love your hair!"

"Thanks!"

Feeling extra chipper after the exchange of compliments, Ria stopped to get ice cream and then walked the rest of the way down to the water. There were benches and stairs facing the dock and she sat down on a step, staring out at the harbor as she enjoyed the ice cream and the moment.

It was much quieter than the Big Apple. Technically Annapolis was a city, but not in the same way as New York. Everything was made of brick; it looked older and less shiny, and there were no skyscrapers. The harbor itself was small, with docks for sailing boats that bobbed in place on the waves. Ducks and seagulls swirled in the air before landing on the water.

One particularly brave seagull landed a few feet in front of her and eyeballed her, reminding her of the pigeons back home. He hopped a little closer and she glared at him, taking a big bite of her ice cream.

"This is mine. Not for you." She kicked her leg toward him, and he hopped back but didn't take flight again. Deciding to ignore the gull, she focused on finishing up her ice cream. Once she was done, the bird flew away.

Pigeons and gulls. Not so different. Good to know.

She pulled out her laptop and took a deep breath. The air smelled different here. A little salty, thanks to the water, and clean and fresh. She could also smell seafood, and it smelled amazing.

One of the things she was apparently definitely supposed to try in Maryland were the crabs and crabcakes. Though she was doubtful they would be all that different from anywhere else, it was a 'thing' according to the internet. Maybe tonight she'd get a crabcake, just so she could say she'd tried one.

Oh, yes! And she could post it to her social media and tell her readers to guess where her next series was going to be set.

Perfect.

But in the meantime, she needed to finish up her *current* series.

Granted, she wasn't feeling very 'big city' at the moment, what with the salt-scented air, the cries of the gulls, and the quiet buzz of people and very few cars behind her. She was used to a lot more noise, but it was nice. Popping open her laptop, she clicked on her document and bent her head to get to work.

A few hours later, she had a crick in her neck and her butt was starting to hurt from sitting on the hard concrete. She'd also written twice as many words as she usually did, though the mental image she'd had of her grumpy hero had slowly morphed into looking an awful lot like Ethan over the course of writing.

It doesn't mean anything.

He was just a hot guy, that was all. He would look great on a book cover though. She snickered, imagining his likely reaction to such a suggestion. There was a reason she didn't tell him what she wrote.

Stretching, she groaned as she got to her feet. Ouch. Too much time sitting today. Thankfully it was going to be a nice little walk back to her car. Maybe she'd go out and walk around again tonight. Only on the main street though. This might not be New York, but she was still going to be careful since she didn't know her way around and she was a woman alone.

Sure, she knew Ethan, sort of, but she didn't have his phone number, so it's not like she could call him if she got into some kind of trouble. She'd have to call Molly so that *she* could call Ethan, and hope that they both picked up. Definitely not ideal.

She should go to the grocery store, but she wasn't really feeling it. It wouldn't hurt her to order dinner in tonight and then go tomorrow morning. Besides, she could offer to order something for Ethan too, maybe sweeten him up a little about having a houseguest.

That was a good idea. Get home early enough to offer to treat him to dinner.

Smiling cheerfully, she headed to her car.

When she got back to the house, he was in the living room watching the news. Guess his workday didn't go *all* day. Molly said he was a translator and he'd traveled a lot in the past but less now, unless it was into D.C.

"Hi," she said, determined to keep things cheerful and upbeat. "How was your day?"

"Pretty good," he replied, lifting his hand in greeting but not actually looking at her. That irked Ria some but she was determined not to let him get under her skin again. "You?"

"Not bad. You were right about New York City."

"I know." He might be focused on the television, but the side of his lip quirked up in smug superiority.

Jerk.

"It's not a bad city though. Though there are a surprising number of places built on former landfills."

"Mmm."

Right. Okay, she'd let him know he was right, time to move on. For her own sanity, she probably shouldn't have brought it up in the first place.

"So, what are you doing for dinner? I was thinking I'd order in and wanted to see if you'd like something too. My treat, obviously."

For the first time, he lifted his head and looked at her—and was it her imagination, or did he look less cranky?

"Oh, thanks. Um, I'm actually going out for dinner tonight. But I appreciate it."

"Right, well, maybe tomorrow. I'm going to stop by the grocery store tomorrow too—I could make us dinner. Is there anything you like in particular?" Oh wait, if he had a date tonight, was he going to think she was trying to get him to go on a date with her tomorrow night? She should probably be clearer. And she was definitely ignoring the little swoop in her stomach that was sad about him going out on a date. That little swoop had no business swooping. "You know, I just feel like I should do something to make up for invading your home."

"Oh. Right." He cracked a smile. "Well, don't worry about that. It's not your fault, and I'll make sure Molly makes it up to me." He got to his feet, turning off the television as he did so. "By the way, I have some groceries being delivered tomorrow and I added some extra staples, as well as some breakfast tea for you."

"Thanks..." Ria watched him, bewildered, as he swept by and headed back to his room. He was so grouchy, but at the same time really considerate, and she didn't know what to make of him.

Well, if he was done working for the day, at least she could take a shower now.

Ethan

"Mary Shelley."

"No, it's Isaac Asimov."

"You know that Mary Shelley wrote *Frankenstein*

decades before Asimov came along right? They asked for the *creator* of science fiction, not the grandfather."

Pierce opened his mouth. Closed it. And glared at Trish, who smirked back at him, tossing one of her long dreads over her shoulder in smug triumph.

"Guys, we're supposed to be competing with the other teams, not each other," Luna said, looking up from where she was writing down their answers to the trivia questions. She had the best handwriting out of all of them, so she always served as their scribe. The one time Ethan had dared to try and write one out while she was in the bathroom, she'd glared at him for the rest of the night after scribbling over his "chicken scratch" and re-writing it.

"Just put Mary Shelley," Jillian told her in a low voice. Her boyfriend Sebastian chuckled. They were the only friends in the group to start dating and actually make it work.

Ethan's gaze flitted over to his own ex, Caitlyn, who was sitting down the table, far away from him. Not because they didn't get along, they got along fine, it had just happened that way. He thought they'd end up like Sebastian and Jillian, maybe even get married one day, but it hadn't worked out.

Neither had Pierce and Trish, although everyone pretended not to know about their one-night drunken hookup since they'd been clear they didn't want to talk about it. *The night that never happened,* was how Luna once described it.

At one point he'd thought Luna and Christian might get together, but for some reason Christian never made a move, and Luna sure as hell wasn't going to. She had confidence about everything except dating. Making the first move was not in her vocabulary.

In some ways, it was kind of a wonder their friend group had lasted as long as it had.

"Okay, once you have your final answers written down, bring up the sheet for this round!" Rob grinned from his place behind the microphone. He ran trivia every Wednesday night and was a familiar figure. They weren't friends, but he was friendly with all the regulars—which Ethan's group was.

This week they'd named themselves *This Episode is called Trivia*. Jillian's nephew had gotten her hooked on a kid show and it was now spreading through their friend group like a disease even though none of them had kids. He'd watched a couple episodes, just to see what it was all about, and had enjoyed it a lot more than he'd thought he would.

"So, I have a houseguest for the next month," he announced. He didn't really know how to segue into it.

"You do? Why didn't you bring them?" Christian asked, frowning across the table at him. With his black hair and tanned skin, his sky-blue eyes were startlingly bright, even in the dim lighting of the bar.

"She's Molly's friend, not mine. Molly offered her room up to her best friend from New York and didn't bother to tell me until this morning—which is when Ria arrived." Ethan rolled his eyes.

"Sounds like Molly," Trish said, laughing. She'd always had a soft spot for his younger sister. Probably because they were both big brats.

"You were nice to her, weren't you, Ethan?" asked Caitlyn. And that was the problem with hanging out with his ex; she knew him way too well.

"Sure." Nice enough anyway. He hadn't pitched a fit and he'd convinced her to stay.

"Why didn't you invite her out with us?" Jillian asked. "Or was she too tired from traveling?"

Ethan shrugged, picking up his beer to take a sip, and feeling more than a little uncomfortable. He'd thought about inviting Ria out, and then changed his mind. He hadn't wanted to. She'd come in all fresh and upbeat, adorably stumbling over her words as she asked if she could order him some food, and he'd needed to get away.

To get some space.

From a woman he'd just met whom he'd barely spent any time with.

Yeah, he really didn't want to examine too closely why he'd felt the need to flee. He had a feeling he wouldn't like the answer.

He hadn't even taken the time to ask her about her pen name, which she must be using because this afternoon he'd searched for every iteration of her real name that he could think of and hadn't come back with a single author.

"Ethan, you should have invited her out," chided Caitlyn, shaking her head.

"Maybe next time."

"Maybe we should just go to his house," suggested Trish with a wicked smile, looking around at everyone but him, as if avoiding his gaze meant he couldn't hear her. "We can introduce ourselves."

"Oh yeah, just a whole group of us descending on her at once, late at night, with no warning. Sounds like a great way to make friends," Pierce said sarcastically.

Trish scowled across the table at him. "I didn't say we should do it *tonight*."

"How about you don't do it at all? Look, if she's free, I'll invite her to the crab feast on Saturday, okay? And if she's not, maybe some other time. She's going back up to New York at the end of the month anyway." Anyone was welcome at a crab feast. Plus, Ria said she wanted to research Maryland. That was the perfect place to do some research. It would also get his friends off his back, and she wouldn't be expecting an invite to his weekly night out or anything. That would be a lot better than taking her to trivia night where she might expect another invitation the following week.

Thankfully his suggestion—and the next round of trivia starting—got everyone off his back. One crab feast. It wouldn't be so bad. And if it gave him a little thrill to have an excuse to invite her to it, no one needed to know that.

CHAPTER 4

Despite her midmorning nap, after unpacking and settling in, Ria had still been so tired that she'd gone to bed early, long before Ethan had returned home. Hopefully his night had gone well. Then he might be in a better mood. And she was not at all jealous of the idea of him going out on a date. Nope. She had no reason to be. The weird feeling in her stomach all evening was just anxiety from being a new place.

Of course, going to bed early meant she was now awake early—although not as early as yesterday thank goodness. She thought about trying to fall back asleep, but her bladder protested immediately.

Nope, bathroom.

She didn't even try to fool herself into thinking that maybe she'd be able to fall back asleep after. Once she was up, she was up, and she knew it.

Ah well.

Still yawning, she let herself out into the hallway,

turning to head for the bathroom... and ran smack into a bare, wet, smelly, but still ridiculously attractive chest.

"Eek!" Ria stumbled back too fast and fell right on her butt, which meant that it was a long, long, long way to look up at Ethan, who was standing over her in running shorts, hands on his hips. Small beads of sweat dewed his skin, glistening in the hallway light, making him look like a well-oiled cover model. It only took a moment for true concern to creep over his face.

"You okay?" he asked, dropping his hands from his hips as he started to bend down, like he was going to touch her.

"Yup, yup, fine." Ria scooted away from his hand, pushing herself to her feet. He stood back up with a bemused expression on his face, his gaze slowly traveling over her and immediately making her feel self-conscious. Was there something wrong with what she was wearing? It was a cute, silky top and short bottoms set, but it wasn't sexy or anything and... oh, well, her nipples might be a little hard. Ria crossed her arms to cover them up. "Are you okay?"

Dragging his gaze up from her legs, he smirked at her.

"I'm fine. I'm not the one who fell over."

"Right. Sorry. Again. I was just headed the bathroom."

"Me too." Of course, he was talking about *his* bathroom, which was in the master bedroom. He ran his hand through his dark hair, leaving it looking attractively windswept. Was there anything this man did that wasn't attractive? Talk about being rough on a girl's libido.

On the other hand, she had a feeling the upcoming sex scene she needed to write was going to be extra spicy.

Especially with all the fodder her imagination was going to have after seeing him in nothing but running shorts.

Ah, shit, she was staring at his chest again.

Ria jerked her gaze up to meet his, blushing furiously as he raised his eyebrow at her.

"So I'm going to go do that now," she blurted out before he could say anything. Then she dodged around him to disappear into the bathroom, ignoring his stupid little chuckle as she went past.

He was still in the shower went she went back to her room—she could hear the water running—and she got ready for the day as quickly as she could, but he still beat her to the kitchen. Thankfully, the awkwardness of running into each other had been fully dispelled, and he just glanced at her when she walked in.

"Want an omelet?" he asked as she entered. He was standing in front of the stove, holding the handle of a pan on it, apparently already cooking one.

"Um, what kind?" She hadn't expected to be offered breakfast.

"What do you want in it?" Gesturing to his left, she realized there was an assortment of possible ingredients on the counter.

"Just ham and cheese, please. Thank you."

"You're welcome." He slid the omelet he'd just finished onto a plate and then put a little more oil in the bottom of the pan.

"Oh..." Ria started forward. "I can make it. You should eat your breakfast."

"I've got it. Sit." He pointed at the counter where she'd sat yesterday. Just as he said the words, the tea kettle on the back of the stovetop began shrilly whistling. This time, Ria didn't move, she just watched aghast as he moved the tea kettle to a different burner, turned off the burner it had been on, and then dropped ham into the omelet pan.

Then, while the ham was heating up, he grabbed a mug out of the cupboard and poured the hot water into it, before turning around and seeing that she was still standing where she had been before. He frowned at her.

"Come sit down, Ria."

Bossy McBossypants.

Yet this time she found herself moving forward, as if his voice had some kind of hypnotic control over her. Talk about embarrassing.

He put the mug down where she'd sat the day before, followed by a box of teabags, and then a little cannister marked 'sugar.' "Do you need milk?"

"Um, no, thank you." She stared at him. The guy didn't even like her, she'd invaded his home, and here he was making breakfast for her and even her morning tea. Her boyfriends hadn't treated her this well. Clearly, she needed to raise her standards, because holy crap. Ethan didn't seem to find anything particularly impressive about what he was doing. He had already turned his back on her, taking a bite of his omelet before pouring some egg mixture into the pan along with her ham.

A few minutes later he was sliding the plate in front of her along with another cannister. This one was a bright yellow metal tin with a red top and blue backing labeled Old Bay.

"Oh, I've seen this when I was researching," Ria said, delighted, as she reached for it. "It's pretty big in Maryland, right?"

Ethan snorted. "You could say that."

"It's for my omelet?" She'd thought it was for crabs, but hey, he was the one who lived here.

"Old Bay is for everything." He tipped his plate towards her and she realized she could see a sprinkling of something red across his entire omelet. Well, okay then. When she sprinkled a little on just the end of her omelet, he frowned at her.

"Just want to make sure I like it before I cover my food in it," she said, feeling the scrutiny of his gaze. Why did it feel like she was being given some kind of test?

She'd felt this way when one of her exes had shown her *Star Wars* for the first time. Like he'd been watching her watch the movies and if she didn't react appropriately she was going home single. They'd broken up later for other reasons, but that memory was coming back forcibly now.

Trying to ignore his uncomfortable stare, she took a bite of egg that was covered in red powder. "Oh!" She stared down at it. "This is good!" She wasn't sure she could describe what it tasted like... It didn't taste like anything she'd ever had before. It was salty, but that wasn't the real essence of the flavor.

Rather than responding, Ethan just nodded, then walked away, carrying his plate and fork with him. Ria stared after him as he went down the hall and disappeared into his office, closing the door behind him. She really couldn't get a read on him; it was like emotional whiplash back and forth between being incredibly thoughtful to being a crabby dick.

What was she supposed to do with that?

Shaking her head, she reached for the Old Bay and added some more to her omelet. Once she was done, she figured she'd get out of the house and out of his hair for a bit. She could do some writing and also go grocery shopping, the way she'd intended to yesterday. Plus, even though she hated to admit it, she really was feeling inspired to churn out the final sex scene after her run-in with Ethan this morning.

Maybe she should make it a shower scene. Dax, her hero, could come in all hot and sweaty after a workout...

Shaking off her increasingly lustful thoughts, Ria cleaned up her dishes—including the pan that Ethan had used to make breakfast—before leaving the house. Her brain wasn't really on the housework though, it was on her story... and not her current one. She couldn't stop thinking about her next book. Her next series. Maybe the first book could be a forced proximity, unexpected house-guest romance.

Or is that a little too on the nose?

It wasn't like she thought Ethan would ever read it.

Molly will though.

Right. Probably shouldn't make it quite so obvious she was lusting after her best friend's brother. Even if it would be cathartic to write a story that fulfilled her current wayward fantasies.

This time she went out with the purpose of finding a coffee shop where she could sit and write. The first part was easy enough, and it was apparently a slow morning so there were plenty of open tables, but she also wanted to make sure she wasn't going to get chased off. This coffee shop was perfect. It was cute and local, a light airy space with low murmurs of conversation but no one being overly loud. Plus, it looked out on the street where she could people watch. Final bonus: it smelled amazing.

Once she put in her order, she gave her best smile to

the cashier, a pretty black woman who looked about Ria's age. Her nametag said 'Trish.'

"Is it okay to grab a table and stay a while?" Ria asked, hefting her laptop bag as if to explain why she was asking. Trish flipped a long dreadlock over her shoulder, glancing down at the bag and then back up at Ria.

"How long is 'a while'?" she asked, a little brisk, but not unfriendly. There was something in her gaze, as she studied Ria's face a lot more intently than Ria expected. It made her feel a little uncomfortable, like Trish was seeing something more than just her. "I don't want to be rude, but we do usually have a lunch rush and management frowns on us letting people who only bought a cup of coffee staying through that. The tables fill up pretty quickly."

"I'll make sure I'm gone for lunch, or I'll order some to eat," she said hastily. She lowered her voice a little. Sometimes admitting the reason helped. "I'm an author and I need a place to write, plus I'm trying to catch more of the sights and sounds of Maryland. I'm here on a research trip."

Trish's eyes lit up with interest and Ria mentally breathed a sigh of relief. This was going to be one of those times when admitting her agenda helped. Some people felt like there was a certain mystique to being an author. Heck, she'd heard about one author who had written a best-selling book based off her experiences writing in the customer service area of a tire shop.

"What do you write?" Trish asked eagerly. "I love to read. I don't think we've had an author in here before. At least, not that I know of."

"Romance," Ria said. She always left off what *kind* of romance when she first talked to someone about it. There were a lot of people who looked down on romance in general, and even more who looked down on the kind of romance she wrote. Daddy Doms were seriously misunderstood.

Something flashed in Trish's eyes, something Ria had seen before at book conventions, but never out in public.

"Oh. My. God. You're Dakota Darling!" Trish squealed, and Ria blushed red hot, feeling lightheaded and yet also incredibly excited.

This was it.

Her first time ever being recognized in public... and she had no idea what to do. She wanted to cheer and hug Trish and run away until she could calm her suddenly pounding heart, all at the same time. It was validating and terrifying and... did she have a book on her? Could she give Trish a copy?

"Sorry, sorry," Trish said, lowering her voice. She was practically quivering behind the counter, which she now gripped hard enough that it looked like she might spring up at any moment. "I didn't mean to just shriek your pen name like that... it's just, I love your books. So do all my friends. You're in Maryland? For a research trip? Does that mean your next series..."

"Will be set in Maryland, yes." Ria grinned, leaning in as she spilled the secret in a whisper. Trish's enthusiasm was undeniable and completely contagious, and it felt so, so amazing.

"Oh. My. God. Come in whenever you want; I promise I'll make sure you aren't bothered." Trish's dark eyes gleamed with excitement. "Do you have any questions? Do you need sources? Wait, do you know anyone here? My friends and I would be happy to talk to you, we all love your books—I said that already didn't I?"

"I never get tired of hearing it," Ria reassured her with a laugh. It was also the truth. "I would *love* to meet your friends. My bestie is from here and I'm staying at her place, but she's actually up in New York, which is where I'm from." This would be perfect. She'd been hoping to make a few acquaintances, at best, in a month's time. Finding a reader who loved her books and wanted to hang and help her out?

Best. Thing. Ever.

"We're getting together for happy hour tomorrow night if you're free," Trish said, grinning. "It's a mix of us. I don't think the guys have read your books, but they're always happy to have another lady come hang out with us, and all my girlfriends are going to lose their shit when I tell them you're coming."

Ria pressed her hand against her chest. "Thank you so much, you have no idea what that means to me." She beamed at Trish, thanking her lucky stars for leading her to this particular coffee shop at this particular time. It felt a little like fate guiding her.

CHAPTER 5

<u>ETHAN</u>

Ria did know how to make herself scarce. Ethan wasn't sure where she was going during the day, and he didn't ask because he didn't want her to think he cared, but she did a good job of disappearing all day. And he definitely did not feel disappointed when he came out of his office on both Thursday *and* Friday to eat lunch and found that he was alone in the house. Feeling disappointed wouldn't make any sense. He *liked* being alone in his house and was grateful she wasn't an obnoxious houseguest, so obviously that wasn't what he was feeling.

But he *was* curious what she was doing. He was still her host after all. And by Friday afternoon, he still hadn't invited her to Saturday's crab feast. So, he really needed to get on that. He didn't have her number though, and he didn't want to ask Molly for it.

His sister had texted a few times to find out how things were going, and Ethan told her things were 'fine' and that he wasn't keeping track of Ria's every movement. So, if he asked for Ria's number, he was sure Molly would give him a hard time about his change of direction. Plus, he didn't really want his sister to know he was going to be inviting Ria to hang out with him and his friends.

If it didn't go well, he didn't want to feel obligated to do it again just to make Molly happy. Considering Ria didn't seem super friendly, he had a feeling tomorrow was going to be super awkward, if she could come at all.

When he heard her come home around four o'clock, he went out to say hi and invite her to the crab feast. Yeah, he'd left it till the last minute, a little, but asking her tomorrow morning would be inexcusably last minute. Asking her the day before felt less rude.

"Oh hey," she said, setting her laptop down on the counter before heading to the cupboard to get out a glass. "How are you?"

"Good," he replied, leaning against the doorframe and watching her. "You?"

She flashed him a smile that was a customer service smile if he'd ever seen one. Talk about fake. Yeah, tomorrow was going to be awkward. He hoped she didn't say yes. Maybe she'd even have plans that would preclude her from coming. Though, hoping for that possibility wasn't why he'd kept putting off asking her.

Really.

"I'm great." She took a long pull of water and glanced at the clock. "I'm in a bit of a hurry though."

"Plans tonight?" His stomach flipped over at the thought that she had a date tonight. It wasn't jealousy, of course. That would make as little sense as being disappointed that she wasn't around during the day for lunch. It was a weird feeling though, one he couldn't immediately pinpoint.

Worry, probably, like he would have for Molly if she

was in a totally new place and had made a date within forty-eight hours.

"Yeah, and I still need to freshen up." She ran her hand over her hair as she took another gulp of water. She looked good to him. The cute little capris she was wearing were covered in cherries and matched the headband holding her hair back. Both went well with her black lacy top. Her makeup still looked freshly applied.

High-maintenance, remember?

It was cute on her though. He couldn't deny that.

"Right, well, I've got plans tonight too." He didn't bother telling her that he was meeting up with friends for happy hour. Not like it was her business anyway. And it definitely wasn't because it was a competition of who had better plans. "But um, my friends and I are having a crab feast tomorrow afternoon if you'd like to come."

"A crab feast?" She perked up immediately. "I would love to. What time?"

"Ah well, we're gonna start around noon." He didn't know what possessed him, because he hadn't meant to include an offer for the morning, but it ended up coming out anyway. "I'm going crabbing in the morning for it, if you want to come with me."

She clutched the glass in front of her, her excited eyes widening to an almost comical degree. The strange feeling in his stomach had changed, but it was still there and getting stranger by the moment. Maybe the sandwich meat he'd had at lunch had gone off.

"I would *love* to go crabbing! I... what do I need to wear?"

Of course, her first thought was about clothes. Though, at least in this case it was a sensible first thought.

"We'll be going out on my boat so sneakers, no heels,

and clothing that won't flap in the wind. No dresses, skirts, scarves, or anything like that. And put your hair back." As he spoke, Ria nodded eagerly, still looking excited. Ethan eyed her speculatively. "Can you swim?"

"I wasn't on a team or anything, but yes."

"You'll wear a life vest the entire time we're out there." Ethan did not fuck around with safety. The fact that she felt the need to qualify her statement meant he wanted the life vest on her body, not just on hand.

"Yes Sir," she said, giving him a mock salute. The weird feeling moved from his stomach to his cock.

Yeah, well. Being called 'Sir' did things to him, though not as much as being called 'Daddy' did. He ignored the twinge and cleared his throat.

"Alright then. I'll be planning to head out around nine, so don't stay out too late." *On your date.* Obviously he left that part unsaid.

"Got it," she replied cheerfully, thankfully not calling him 'Sir' again.

"Great. Well, I'll see you then." He had a few more emails he wanted to respond to before he headed out to meet his friends.

It just so happened that when he came out of his office, she was coming out of her room —and yes, she'd freshened up. Her cherry capris and lace top had been replaced by a cute black dress that was covered in more cherries. She'd added some chunky jewelry, and her hair was bouncing around her shoulders in soft waves. She looked damn good.

"Oh hey, you're headed out now too?" she asked, blinking up at him through ridiculously long lashes.

"Yeah." He grunted the word. Something about the way she'd gotten all dolled up for this date was really getting under his skin. Part of him wanted to ask if she even knew the guy or if she'd taken any safety precautions, the way he would with Molly, but Ria wasn't his sister and she was an adult. She could make her own choices. But there was one thing he could do. "You should give me your phone number."

"What?" She stared at him.

"You should give me your number. And I'll give you mine. In case we need to contact each other at any point." Like if her date went south or her car broke down or something.

"Oh... right, well I guess that makes sense." She gave her head a little shake, looking at him suspiciously, though he didn't know why. Though, perhaps he should have asked for her number instead of demanding it.

They exchanged numbers and headed out to their respective cars. Ethan let her go first, like a gentleman, then followed her down the street. They both turned right. It was a little weird coming up right behind her, but eventually they would go in different directions.

Except they didn't.

She made every turn he did before him, making him look like a freaking stalker all the way to the parking lot of the restaurant. When she got out of her car, she gave him a look of disbelief, which he returned.

"This is where you're meeting your friends?"

"Yeah." He eyed her. "Well, I guess we should go in."

And since he was a gentleman and held the door open for her, he ended up following her into the restaurant too. He wasn't so much a gentleman that he didn't step around her when she slowed down at the host desk though. His friends always took over the same table for happy hour, so he knew exactly where he was going.

He was normally one of the first ones to show up, but today all the girls were already there. Pierce was already there too; he was a stickler for being on time and tended to arrive to everything at least ten minutes early.

"What's everyone doing here already?" Ethan asked, sliding into one of the open seats.

"Trish met one of our favorite authors at the coffee shop. She's here to research Maryland," Luna said brightly, brimming with excitement. There was an odd swooping sensation in Ethan's stomach. *No fucking way. It couldn't be.*

"Oh my God, there she is!" Trish stood up, waving her hand over her head at someone back near the entrance. "Over here, Dakota!"

Not Ria, not Ria, not Ria...

But Ethan already knew the answer before he turned around.

Ria wasn't out on a date tonight. She was here to meet his friends.

Of all the bars in all the world...

Her gaze met his as she moved toward the table, and she quirked a small smile at him. Ethan sighed inwardly and turned around to try and catch the server's eye. He needed a drink and he needed it fast.

<u>*Ria*</u>

Ethan's friends were very nice, even if he wasn't. Not that he was being mean or anything, but he sure wasn't welcoming either. Ria felt kind of bad. She hadn't meant to take over his home, or his group of friends, without warning.

The table had divided into two sides. She was at one end with all the other women, Ethan was at the other with all the men. The guys were mostly having their own conversation, while she and the women talked about the obvious topic—books. It looked like the only couple were Jillian and Sebastian, though she'd seen a few heated glances passed between Trish and Pierce too. But they were seated far apart from each other, across the table, and didn't interact much.

Ria was sitting in between Trish and Caitlyn, who had both proclaimed themselves to be her biggest fans. She was just as fascinated by them as they were by her. In fact, the whole group of friends was an eclectic mix and she loved seeing their differences and similarities.

For instance, three of them were wearing things with the Maryland flag on them. Ethan had his sunglasses, which were now perched on top of his head, Caitlyn had on a shirt with a large crab on her chest that was colored in with the flag rather than a single color, and Jillian had on a bracelet with the flag's colors. Hearing that Marylanders had a thing for their flag and seeing it were two very different things, she realized.

On top of that, Sebastian was wearing a shirt that said, "Fear the Turtle" and had a cartoon turtle holding a flag with a large M on it. She could only assume that was something about the state as well, but she didn't know what. She'd always associated Maryland with crabs, not turtles.

And for good reason, because the crabcakes were amazing. She'd had 'Maryland-style' crab cakes in New York before, and while she could not pinpoint the difference, it was there. Maybe it was just the amount of crab in them, but she had a feeling the seasoning had something to do with it too, and she was pretty sure it was Old Bay. She felt jazzed about knowing that, like she had insider information.

Leaning over to Caitlyn, she nodded toward Sebastian. "What does 'fear the turtle' mean?"

"Oh, it's from the University of Maryland. We all went there; that's how we met. The terrapin is the school's mascot."

Ria took that in for a moment. Nope. She was still confused. "Aren't terrapins and turtles different?"

Caitlyn and Trish snickered.

"Damn right, and if you call Testudo a turtle, we'll always correct you." Trish grinned at Ria's obvious confusion. "But Fear the Turtle has better flow than Fear the Terrapin."

"Plus, it confuses our enemies." Jillian quipped, turning her head to join in their conversation. She'd been going back and forth a little between the guys' conversation and theirs.

"You have enemies?" Ria couldn't help but be amused. Was this part of Maryland culture too?

"Well, Duke."

"*Fuck Duke.*"

Ria jumped as literally everyone at the table said it at the exact same time, like it was a reflex. They weren't the only ones either, it echoed through the restaurant from multiple patrons. Her jaw dropped open as everyone else just kept going on with their conversations as if nothing had happened and they hadn't all done a Greek chorus of expletives.

"Can I ask a kind of personal question?" Luna, for all that she seemed shy, had actually asked a lot of the more probing questions already.

Shaking off her shock at the odd response to just hearing the word "Duke," Ria smiled encouragingly at her. "Sure."

She'd gotten all dressed up for tonight because she'd wanted to look good and feel good and look the part of whatever they might picture for Dakota Darling, but she'd settled in really quickly. They all were calling her Ria now and it felt more like talking with a group of friends than fans, even though they were talking about her books.

"Well," Luna glanced around at the others, as if looking for approval. "I'll tell you something personal too. We're all involved in the scene and we've been so impressed with how you portray the kink aspect in your writing, and I was wondering if you have any firsthand experience that you're writing from or if it's research or just your imagination. Not that there's anything wrong with just your imagination," she added hastily. "It just seems like there's more to it."

Of course, the guys' side of the table fell silent while Luna was asking the question, and they were now paying a lot more attention to the conversation happening with Ria. Even though she kept her focus on Luna, she could practically feel Ethan's gaze on her, waiting for her answer to the question.

She had no idea how much he'd been listening in, but surely by now he'd picked up that she wrote extra-spicy romance, even if he didn't know it was kinky or Daddy Dom.

Wait, did Luna just say they're all involved in the scene? Ethan too?

Oh dear.

Her brain was going to be obsessing over that later.

In the meantime, she needed to answer the question.

It wasn't the first time someone had asked her, in fact it was one of the questions she'd been asked the most, so she had her answer well-rehearsed. "It's from research and my imagination," she admitted. "I read one book, got hooked, and when I started writing it was mostly from all of that. I know clubs exist in New York, but I've never gotten the courage to go to one by myself."

"Ever wanted to try it for real?" Christian leaned forward on the table, bracing himself against strong forearms as a lazy smile spread across his face.

"Absolutely not." Ethan scowled at Christian and then at her, as if she'd been the one to answer, and Ria's mouth dropped open in shocked indignation.

CHAPTER 6

Should have kept my mouth shut. He clenched his jaw, but it was already too late. He hadn't thought before speaking, which wasn't like him, but when Christian made his offer, he'd reacted. He couldn't help himself.

Now Ria was glaring at him from the other side of the table. "And why not?" she asked, narrowing her eyes at him.

Shit. Ethan's mind raced for a good excuse that didn't include the admission that he didn't want his friend putting his hands all over her. "Christian isn't a Daddy Dom. You write Daddy Dom romances, right?"

"Hey, a spanking is a spanking," Christian said, laughing. He turned to meet Ethan's gaze and Ethan glared at him before letting his gaze slide over to Luna, who was suddenly very focused on her cheese fries. Christian looked over as well, and immediately subdued. He cleared his throat and faced Ria again. "But I mean, it would probably be better to get firsthand experience from an actual Daddy Dom. Did you know that Ethan is one?"

That fucker. Talk about throwing him under the bus.

Ethan couldn't help but glance at Caitlyn, to see how she was taking all of this, but she was grinning at Ria now and not looking at him at all.

"Oh, Ethan would be a great choice to help you research. I can vouch for him. He's very good."

Part of him appreciated the vote of confidence, the other part of him wanted to know why the hell his ex thought it was appropriate to pimp him out to her favorite author for research purposes. What was happening to his life?

Ria blinked at Caitlyn like she was trying to parse out exactly what Caitlyn meant. "You vouch for him?" she asked faintly.

"Well, yeah. He's my ex. But we're still friends. And if you're looking for a Daddy Dom to talk to, Ethan is a great choice. Though, Christian is the only Dom at this table who isn't a Daddy, but I can't personally vouch for any of them." Caitlyn snickered, glancing over at Trish, who looked up to study the ceiling rather than give Pierce a similar recommendation.

Ethan closed his eyes, taking another long swig of his drink and suppressing the groan that was building inside him. This was not how he'd seen his night going. And yet, now he couldn't stop picturing putting Ria over his knee and lifting up that cute little cherry- covered skirt to find out what she was wearing underneath.

Fuck me sideways.

"So you're his Old Bae?" Ria snickered and the table erupted with laughter.

Even Ethan couldn't help joining in, and this time he couldn't hold back the groan, because that was an awful pun.

But also really fucking cute.

Why did she have to be so damned cute and attractive?

His and Caitlyn's friendship had never fully recovered after their break-up. As amicable as it had been, Ethan had learned his lesson about fucking too close to home. And Ria was actually living in his home. Getting involved, in any capacity, was a horrible idea.

Maybe on the last week she was here, when she was about to go home anyway, but definitely not before then.

"Ria and I are doing research tomorrow—not that kind—" He shot a look at Sebastian, who snickered. He needed to shift the subject before things got even more out of hand. "She's going crabbing with me in the morning and then I invited her to the afternoon crab feast."

Jillian clapped her hands in excitement. "That's right! I forgot we told you to invite Molly's friend to that! Or maybe I hit a disconnect between Molly's friend and Dakota Darling... whatever. Yay!" She beamed at Ria. "I'm so glad you're coming. We'll be able to answer any questions you want. Oh, and we'll bring some more Maryland stuff for you to try!"

"Like what?" Ria asked curiously, clearly not realizing what she was getting herself into.

"Like a Smith Island cake. We'll go grab one in the morning," Jillian replied, ignoring Sebastian's groan, even though it was well justified. It wasn't like the bakery was that close to where they lived, but Jillian loved Smith Island cake and jumped at any excuse to get them.

"Oh, and Berger cookies! I can bring those," Trish volunteered.

"I've got the lemons and peppermint sticks!" Caitlyn

laughed at Ria's expression. "Don't knock it till you've tried it."

"I'll get the Natty Boh." Christian grinned. "Don't worry, I'll bring other beer too, but she needs to at least try it."

"Is everything food related?" Ria asked, clearly amused.

"For a crab feast it is." Pierce looked at Ethan. "She needs to go to an O's game too."

It was on the tip of Ethan's tongue to retort that she could handle that herself, but he also didn't want any of his friends jumping in to offer to take her places either.

Fucking hell, he needed to get a grip.

"Oh, we should all go together," Caitlyn said, saving him rather than throwing him under the bus this time. "That would be so much fun. It's been forever since we've gone to a game."

Everyone else agreed. And then added on that Ria should come to trivia with them on Wednesday. No one seemed to notice Ethan glowering at the end of the table as she was invited to invade more and more of his life. At the same time, he secretly liked knowing that he was going to get to see more of her. She was getting under his skin in a way he didn't understand, but couldn't deny either. Not if he was being honest with himself.

He was attracted to her. He wanted to spend more time with her. He just also knew it was a fucking bad idea and so it was making him crabby as hell.

At the end of the night, they all left as a group, the guys following behind the women into the parking lot, making sure they got safely to their cars. All of them were bunched up around Ria, giggling and talking, obviously thrilled to have her as part of their group. Ethan stood and watched, arms crossed over his chest, as they hugged her goodbye.

Great. Now she was not only living with him, she'd be hanging out with his friends all month too. Hugging meant she'd been accepted into the group and the ladies were going to invite her everywhere, regardless of how he felt. She was going to be unavoidable.

So maybe just give in? You could show her what it's like to have a Daddy Dom. It's only a month. Less than. What could go wrong in less than a month?

It didn't sound like she's done anything kinky before. A lot could go wrong. Stop thinking with your dick.

What if she likes it?

What if he needed to stop thinking in circles because it wasn't like she'd expressed any interest in actually trying anything anyway?

She glanced at him as the little group broke up and she headed for her car. Ethan gave her a wave and got into his car before her, but then waited for her to pull out so he could follow her home. Everyone had stopped after a couple of drinks and had plenty of food and water, but he still felt compelled to make sure she got back to the house safely.

<u>Ria</u>

Finally back in Molly's room, Ria sat down on the bed and let out a breath. She could hear Ethan moving around outside the closed door, though she wasn't entirely sure what he was doing. She'd retreated to the bedroom as soon as they got home, not really sure how to face him alone with all her new knowledge. It had been easier to not think about when they were at the bar with everyone else, in the middle of conversation.

Now that it was just the two of them, she couldn't stop her brain from racing with inappropriate thoughts.

He's a Daddy Dom! He could help with research!

Oh, is that what we're calling it now?

Hey, I've always wanted to do hands-on research.

With your best friend's brother? That's a recipe for disaster.

Or for a romance novel.

Yeah, except that you're not looking for romance, remember?

Romance no, but she wouldn't object to an orgasm or two... Her whole body flushed as she remembered the way Ethan looked at her from across the table while they were talking about 'research.' He'd seemed a little appalled that his ex-girlfriend was recommending his services, but he also hadn't rejected the idea. And he hadn't wanted Christian to help her out.

What did it all mean?

Probably that he's attracted to you, but he doesn't want to be attracted to you.

Right. Well. They were in the same boat then.

But why couldn't they have some fun while she was in town?

Molly.

Would Molly care?

Ria considered the question for a moment. She wasn't sure. She didn't think so.

Does Molly need to know?

Now that might be a better question.

It wasn't like she'd have to tell her. Ria didn't normally keep secrets from Molly, but sometimes there were things that were better not talked about. A fling with Molly's brother... would Molly even want to know?

But how would Ethan feel about that?

Getting up, Ria let out a long sigh before getting herself ready for bed. She got into her pajamas, then peeked out the door to make sure the hallway was empty before scurrying to the bathroom to do her skincare routine and brush her teeth. She did the same thing on the way back.

By the time she closed Molly's bedroom door behind herself, her heart was pounding, and she had to shake her head at her own silliness. It wasn't like Ethan would be able to know her thoughts just from looking at her. He wouldn't know she was thinking about the fact that he was a Daddy Dom and lusting after him even more than she already had been.

Right?

She'd figured out he was attracted to her though. At least, she was pretty sure. It was not impossible that he'd also figured out she was attracted to him.

As she was getting into bed, she heard more noise out in the hallway, almost like he'd been waiting for her to shut herself in her room before he went out there again.

Is he avoiding me?

Maybe.

Turning off the light, she lay down in the bed and stared up at the ceiling as her eyes slowly adjusted. She closed them. But it didn't help her feel sleepier. In fact, it was worse because now all she could see was Ethan's face. His glower. His incredible shirtless torso after she'd run into him in the hallway and the way his hipbones had dipped into his running shorts...

With a groan, Ria gave in to the inevitable.

One hand slid into her top, the other under her bottoms and underwear. Legs bent as she spread them apart, shuddering as she stroked her fingers over the slick wetness gathered between them. Her other hand cupped her breast, pinching the already hardened nipple.

She was way more turned on than she should be considering nothing had happened. Sometimes she got this aroused when she was actually writing, but not normally from just picturing a man. On the other hand, she'd never met a real-life Daddy Dom before either.

Not that she was picturing any of the other guys at the table tonight that were also Daddy Doms. Nope. Ethan was the one her brain had locked in on, it was his face and body fueling her fantasy.

His knee that she was imagining being turned over.

Had she ever been spanked?

Nope.

But she could imagine he would be good at it. Slowly heating her skin, his shirt sleeves rolled up to his elbows, his hand coming down again and again on her upturned bottom while she squirmed and squealed. The other hand would hold her wrists in the small of her back, immobilizing her... and then he'd put her on her knees and grip her by her hair, bringing her forward to take Daddy's cock in her mouth to finish her apology while her backside burned and throbbed, her pussy clenching between her thighs because naughty girls don't get orgasms...

Ria moaned, shuddering, as she rubbed her clit harder, gasping at the intensity of the fantasy. Maybe it was because she finally had a real man she could focus on, instead of an ephemeral dream man, but this fantasy felt so much more substantial than any she'd had in the past.

Her brain flipped a switch, and she was still on her

knees, but no longer with a cock in her mouth. No, Daddy was pounding into her from behind, his hands gripping her hips, his thumb sliding inexorably toward her forbidden entrance...

She rubbed her clit harder, her hips lifting upward as her climax began to spill over her, merging with the fantasy.

"Oh... oh Daddy... oh fuck, Daddy!" Ria shuddered, panting as she hit her peak, the waves of pleasure pulsing through her as her pussy clenched emptily, aching to be filled. "Oh... fuck..."

Slowing her motions, she found that her eyelids were a lot heavier than before. All the tension had drained from her.

"Wow," she whispered. Maybe she didn't need the actual man, the fantasy was pretty damn good.

Ethan

Standing outside Ria's door, leaning against the door frame, Ethan pressed his hand against the throbbing bulge at the front of his pants and closed his eyes, trying to breathe shallowly enough that she didn't hear him out here being a creeper. He'd meant to knock, to check on her, make sure she was feeling okay after his friends had basically word vomited all over her... then he'd heard her calling out for "Daddy" in a passion- filled voice.

He should have walked away immediately.

He shouldn't have stood there, listening to her.

Wishing it was *him* she was calling out for.

Fuck.

CHAPTER 7

<u>ETHAN</u>

Ria in her tight-fitted t-shirt and equally tight capris was dangerous to his focus. Even the lifejacket he'd put on her didn't do anything to lessen how attractive she was. Or maybe it was because he couldn't look at her without hearing her voice ringing in his ears again.

Oh Daddy!

"Wow, it is beautiful out here! Is the Chesapeake Bay Bridge anywhere around here?" Ria asked, turning her head this way and that. Today's outfit was in the theme of blue and white. Blue jean capris with a blue and white wide-striped shirt. The blue and white scarf tied around the base of her ponytail fluttered in the wind along with her hair. Her gold sunglasses stood out against all the navy-and-white stripes.

"No." Ethan couldn't help but shake his head as they pulled up alongside the first crab pot and he killed the motor. "I'll make sure you see it before you leave Maryland. If you have time, you should definitely visit Ocean City. That's more of an overnight trip though."

"Okay. What are you doing?" Ria scooted around to peer into the water as he lowered the crab trap in.

"We're putting the traps in. See this little cage in the center with the fish? That's the bait. The crabs go in through here." He pointed at the opening in the cage, which was broad with a frame, leading to a tunnel that narrowed and ended in pointy wire. "It's shaped this way so they can get in, but not get back out."

"How long does that take?" she asked.

"A few hours. What we're going to do is drop a trap here and then go around putting down a few more. We'll do a loop around to pick them back up. If we don't have enough crabs, we'll pick some up from the store... though with all the extra food everyone is bringing for you, we probably won't need as many crabs as usual."

"Sorry about that, by the way," Ria said as he tossed the cage off the side of the boat and into the water. It started sinking quickly.

"About what?" he asked, turning toward her.

She was watching the disappearing trap with interest before she looked up at him again. "About interrupting your night with your friends. I don't have to keep coming to stuff after today, if you don't want me to." She gave him a nervous smile. "I won't be hurt. I know you didn't expect to share your house, much less your friends."

The fact that she was apologizing and offering to step away actually made him feel better about it all. It was like someone acknowledging that he had a right to be upset made him less so. Plus, did he really want her to stop spending time with him after what'd he'd overheard last night?

Nope.

Not really.

"It's fine. They like you." He maneuvered the boat away from the buoy before kicking up the speed. "I'm sure it will help with your research too."

The sound of the motor was loud, but not so loud they couldn't talk over it if they raised their voices. They'd been silent on the way out—he'd gotten the impression Ria was enjoying being out on the water—but now she scooted closer so she could talk to him.

"Speaking of my research, I've been thinking..."

Her voice trailed off and Ethan glanced over at her. She was blushing hotly, and even though she was wearing sunglasses and he couldn't be sure, he felt like she was staring at his shoulder rather than looking him in the face.

Research. Hands-on. Daddy Doms. Caitlyn pimping him out.

Wait... she wasn't really considering...

"I really never have gotten any firsthand experience with a Dom, much less a Daddy Dom. I could probably use some, to help make my books more realistic."

That did it. Ethan killed the motor. There was no way he was having this conversation shouting over a boat motor. Of course, as soon as he did that, Ria blushed even harder, no longer able to look in his general direction much less meet his gaze and directed her gaze out to the water.

"You want me to show you what it's like to have a Daddy Dom?" He couldn't believe his ears. Sure, he'd heard her last night when she'd obviously been masturbat-ing, but that was a big stretch to 'hey she wants to try this with *me*.'

"Well, yeah. If you'd be interested in that." Her leg jiggled up and down as she managed to return her gaze to his general direction. "I could use some hands-on experience. And I feel like we're both attracted to each other, though feel free to correct me if I'm wrong. But, kink doesn't have to be sexual right? So even if you're not attracted to me, maybe you could help me out anyway?"

She talked so fast it took his brain a moment to catch up to everything she was saying, and he blinked in astonishment.

"Oh, I'm definitely attracted to you." Great, of course those were the first words he managed to form coherently. But she'd caught him off guard, and he didn't do great when he was caught off guard. Unfortunately, that seemed to be her MO. He cleared his throat. "What did you want to... research?"

Great, now his dick was getting hard over the word 'research.'

One shoulder lifted and fell nonchalantly, though her bright red cheeks gave her away.

"You know... what kinds of rules a Daddy Dom might have so I know what it's like to follow them. Consequences for breaking the rules. That kind of thing." Her tongue flicked out against her lower lip and she looked away again.

"Consequences like writing lines? Or spankings?" Fuck, his hand itched to spank her rounded ass. And his erection was only growing at this point. He reached down to adjust himself, which made her drop her gaze, before she snapped her head back to looking away again.

He hadn't thought she could blush any harder, but the pink was now creeping down her neck to her chest.

Damn, that was cute. And fun. Considering how much she'd thrown him off kilter since her arrival, the turnabout was highly enjoyable.

"Whatever you feel is appropriate." Her voice was

higher than it had been before, a cute little squeak that made him grin. She uncrossed and recrossed her legs, squirming slightly in her seat.

Oh, this was going to be fun.

Ethan stepped forward so that he was standing with his feet on either side of hers, and her head snapped back to look up at him. He reached down and plucked the sunglasses off her face, pushing his own to the top of his head at the same time, so he could meet her gaze. He dropped hers on the padded seat next to her, still holding her gaze, while she stared up at him, frozen in place like the prey she now was.

If they were both having the same idea, how bad could it be?

<u>Ria</u>

She couldn't breathe.

It wasn't that Ethan was scary, but he was intimidating, especially when he leaned down over her, his eyes locked on hers, until his lips were hovering mere inches above hers. His hands came down on either side of her body, bracing himself on the back of the bench she was sitting on. The boat rocked slightly, and he moved with it easily, swaying over her.

This morning when he walked out in his Maryland state flag swim trunks and a black shirt that fit over him like a glove, she'd been highly amused. Somehow he managed to make even that look hot, but it was also silly. Then they'd gotten out on the boat and his competence had made him hot again.

She hadn't been able to stop thinking about the idea

of doing Daddy Dom research with him. Watching him maneuver the boat, taking care of the crab traps... Sure his hands smelled a little fishy right now and yet she still wanted them on her. That was saying something.

"Okay, little girl," he said, and her breath hitched in her throat. None of her boyfriends had ever called her that before, and it made all her insides clench in a shocking manner. "I'll be your Daddy while you're here. Agreed?"

Ria nodded her head, feeling suddenly dizzy with the invasion of her space, and yet she didn't want him to go away either.

"First rule: we tell Molly nothing."

"Agreed." She squeaked the word, sounding nothing like herself, which was a little humiliating. "Molly doesn't need to know."

"Good." The slow smile that spread across his lips was devastating, and if she wasn't frozen in place, she might have gone all melty right there on the bench. "Rule number two: we don't tell my friends."

"Got it." That made sense. Going by how everyone had acted last night, they'd give him a really hard time if they knew. Ria didn't particularly want to be teased about it either.

Secret Daddy Dom.

Oo, now that was a promising book title. Or would Secret Daddy be better? No, that sounded like a secret-baby romance.

"Hey." Ethan caught her chin between his fingers, his eyes narrowing as he studied her face.

Oops. Caught with her mind wandering.

"Are you paying attention to me?"

"Yup. Definitely."

He raised one eyebrow at her, and her stomach made a funny dipping sensation. Oh...

"Yes... Daddy." The words felt foreign on her tongue and a flutter of excitement went through her when she said them. The heat that flared in his eyes made her want to say it again.

"Good girl."

He straightened back up and she wanted to cry. Or grab him and pull him back down on top of her. She wanted to press her hands between her legs to relieve some of the ache now throbbing there.

Instead, she grabbed her sunglasses and jammed them back on her face while he smirked at her.

"Now we're going to finish setting the crab traps," he said, returning to his place at the wheel. "Tonight, we'll go over more rules and consequences and your limits."

Tonight. Right. That made sense. Because they should have a thorough discussion before actually doing anything. She knew he was right. At least he was as uncomfortable as she was. He was flying a flag in his flag trunks for the next ten minutes, until they finally reached where he wanted to drop the trap.

This time Ria was the one to toss it in the water, and she grinned watching it go down. This wasn't so bad.

It did get harder when they went back around to pick *up* the traps. Ethan had her do the first one. It wasn't too difficult getting it all the way to the surface, but she also wasn't used to a whole lot of physical labor, and her arms did ache. That wasn't the hard part though. Nor was the fact that her cute little outfit got wet while she was doing it.

The real challenge was when she realized Ethan planned to put the crabs all together in a cooler.

Alive.

Ria's jaw dropped open.

"You're just stacking them on top of each other?" she asked, unable to look away as he began pulling them from the trap and tossing them in the cooler. They were very pretty in a way, with a greenish-blue shell, lighter blue legs, and their pinchers tipped with the red color she normally associated with crabs. They were also a lot smaller than they seemed in the aquariums at the grocery store.

He glanced at her.

"Yeah. You know we're cooking and eating them soon, right?" he asked, eyeing her warily.

"Well... yeah... but..." She hadn't really given much thought to how they'd be treated beforehand. She never had to face that part. Food showed up in the grocery store or the restaurant and she ate it. She'd seen lobsters in the aquarium at the grocery store before and for some reason she now realized that if she *had* thought about transporting them, that's what she would have thought of.

To her surprise, Ethan glanced at the bottom of one of the crabs and then threw it back.

"What was wrong with that one?" she asked, surprised.

"It's a female. We leave those to keep making more little crabs for us to eat." He winked at her.

"So we only eat the males?"

"Well, my friends and I do. Not everyone follows the same rules. But if we want more crabs to keep producing, we've gotta do certain things. Like keeping the bay clean and making sure the females exist to reproduce."

Huh.

For some reason, the fact that they'd only be eating male crabs made her feel a little better.

By the time they got to the sixth trap, she was feeling more sanguine about the crabs in the cooler. Every time they opened it up to add more, they just seemed to be resting inside, much calmer than before, and they didn't seem to care about being stacked on top of each other. In fact, they kept climbing over each other.

That also made her feel a little better.

Right up until a few dropped out of the cage *next* to the cooler rather than *in* it.

"Oh god!" she screamed, jumping back, leaving Ethan to hold the cage by himself—which he probably didn't have any trouble with anyway, but it was easier with two people.

The little crabs started scuttling, waving their pinchers in the air like angry weapons. Now she was really glad she'd followed Ethan's rule about closed-toed shoes, but she still didn't want them getting anywhere near here.

"Just scoop them up from behind," Ethan said, giving her a look as he demonstrated with one hand, still holding onto the trap with the other. "If you need to, step on him from behind – not too hard – and then you can pick him up more easily."

"Eek!" She danced to the side to avoid the crab that was coming right for her, waving its pinchers which looked far more menacing than they had any right too consider how much bigger she was than it. It was obviously the one that Ethan expected her to pick up, but how was she supposed to do that without getting pinched? It moved with her, following her, and she shrieked again. "It's trying to get me!"

Ethan was no help. It was the first time she'd ever heard him really *laugh*. Considering the situation, she did not truly appreciate it the way she might have otherwise.

She and the crab danced around each other, rocking the boat, and Ethan stopped laughing.

"Just pick him up, Ria!" he barked out.

Heart pounding, Ria managed to step over the crab and then put her foot down on its back. Trapped, its pincers waved even more wildly. She scooped it up, the way Ethan had said, wincing as she touched the hard shell. It was wet and cool, and her stomach churned as she tossed it into the cooler—not because she didn't care, but because she didn't want to be touching it anymore.

"Good girl," Ethan said, grinning at her.

She glared at him.

CHAPTER 8

RIA

The day had started out so well.

Then there were crabs and it started to take a turn.

She hadn't known it at the time, but that was the beginning of the descent into utter Maryland madness.

By the time she and Ethan arrived at Pierce's house for the crab feast, she'd mostly gotten over having a cooler full of live crabs in the back of the truck. It just was what it was. And she'd started to feel her spirits lift when everyone greeted them and got her a beer. Natty Boh wasn't really to her taste, it turned out, but she appreciated being included in the experience.

Though she did wish someone had told her there was a dress code.

Ethan was not alone in his Maryland-state-flag apparel. All of his friends were wearing something with the flag on it. Caitlyn was the most decked out. Her hat and sunglasses had the flag, but her t-shirt had an eagle holding what looked like a mallet and a little knife in its claws and instead of a body it had a cannister of Old Bay.

The writing above and below it pronounced: "Land of the Free; Home of Old Bay." When Ria glanced down, she realized that Caitlyn's flipflops were also the Maryland flag.

And yeah, maybe they were all messing with her by wearing all their flag clothing, but that meant that they did already own all of it. None of it looked brand new. They'd all had it just hanging around and had worn it in the past.

Even if it had been new, that would mean they'd been able to run out to the store and get it that quickly.

Marylanders have a thing for their flag is an understatement.

Underscored by the fact that the Natty Boh she was handed was encased in a flag koozie.

That part was cute.

But then the crabs.

Again.

"Oh my God... they're screaming!" Ria covered her ears, watching in horror, as Pierce and Christian tossed crabs into the giant pot they were using, and actual teeny-tiny screams echoed inside the metal cannister of death. They were shaking Old Bay over the crabs and then putting in more.

"No, it's just the air escaping from inside their shells, I promise you they are *not* screaming," Ethan said, putting his arm around her shoulders. Despite seeing the nudge that Caitlyn gave Luna at his action, Ria didn't try to push him away because she needed the reassurance and bracing arm. Pierce put the last crab in and put the lid on the pot. Ria shuddered, hoping that was the end of it.

She wasn't sure she was going to be able to eat any of

these crabs. She eyed the pot of doom. "Are you sure? Because it sounds like they're screaming."

"Crabs don't have vocal chords," he said firmly. "They do have air pockets. And—"

Whatever he was going to say was lost as the top of the pot suddenly clattered to the side, falling to the ground with a loud clang, and crabs began jumping out of the pot.

Now Ria was the one screaming.

Chaos reigned.

She jumped backwards, tearing herself away from Ethan's arm. Everyone else ran forward, bending over to actually try to scoop up the crabs. Ria watched in horror as the crabs—who were just doing their best to escape with their lives—were tossed back into the pot... and started screaming all over again.

"Whoops, forgot to clamp the lid," Pierce said cheerfully.

"You okay there, Ria?" Jillian asked, coming up beside her and looking at her curiously.

"I'm not used to this much excitement when cooking a meal," Ria replied faintly, but really, she was holding back the urge to ask how any of them managed to even think about eating crabs. Ever. But they were all acting like this was completely normal. No big deal. "I don't think I've ever been in danger of my meal trying to pinch me either."

Jillian giggled. "Oh, don't worry. They're easy enough to evade. And those little pincer-armed lunches are going to be delicious when they're done." She grinned widely.

"Right..." Ria found that she was not reassured. Was this what it felt like walking into a cult? Or was *she* the weird one?

"It's not usually this exciting, they don't normally get out of the pot," Ethan said cheerfully. "Come on, we need to get the tables set up with newspaper."

Numbly, Ria joined in with spreading the newspaper out over the huge table that had been set up in Pierce's backyard. She could feel Ethan's eyes on her, watching her with concern. Just like a Daddy Dom would. She wished that made her feel a little better, but right now she was too overcome with crab-induced trauma to enjoy such a little thing.

Thankfully, there was no more excitement, and about fifteen minutes later everyone was sitting at a table littered with the now very dead, red, sprinkled-liberally-with-Old- Bay crabs spread out across the surface. Ria sat in the middle of the bench, staring at the one that was looking back at her, while everyone started grabbing their mallets and tearing at the little bodies.

She winced at the first crack.

Her stomach rumbled.

They did smell delicious, but she wasn't sure she could handle actually eating one... especially seeing what she had to do to get at it. Crab cakes were so much easier to eat.

There was also a bunch of corn on the cob, which looked delicious. Ria grabbed one of those and put it on her plate and then looked over the crabs, trying to appear like she was trying to decide which one she wanted to eat. She really needed them to stop looking back at her.

The crunching and cracking sounds with the mallets and crackers and knives... it sounded torturous. And yeah, she knew the crabs were dead, but it hadn't been that long since she'd heard their little screams.

"Oh, hey Ria, do you need help?" Luna asked from

across the table as she dropped pieces of crab that she'd just pulled out of the shell on Caitlyn's plate. For the first time, Ria noticed that Luna had hot dogs on her plate, rather than any crabs.

She wanted a hot dog. Why did Luna get to eat a hot dog?

"Um, yes?" Ria responded, though she wasn't entirely sure what Luna meant. She didn't think Luna meant help getting a hot dog, though that was currently the help she truly wanted.

"I love picking crabs, but I don't actually like eating crabs," Luna said cheerfully, reaching into the table and grabbing one. Wait, so she didn't like to eat them, she just liked tearing them apart and pulling out their insides?

And that was considered normal?

Christian—who was sitting on Luna's other side—snorted, shaking his head, and squeezing a crab leg between the metal prongs of his cracker until it snapped. "Yeah, she's a bad Marylander," he joked. "If I hadn't seen her birth certificate, I'd have to question whether or not she's actually from here."

"Hey, at least I don't think Wawa is superior to Sheetz."

The roar of noise as everyone suddenly started throwing out their opinion on the matter made Ria jump. It was too hard to pick out what any one person was saying, because they were all talking at once. She didn't even know what they were talking about.

Glancing next to her at Ethan, who was the only one not joining in, she winced as he picked up another crab and began to crack it open.

"Aaaah," she said in a tiny voice. "Ow, that hurt."

Ethan froze. Blinked. Stared down at the crab he was holding. Slowly turned his head to glare at her.

She smiled weakly back at him.

Oops.

But hey, now he knew how she felt.

Shaking his head, he returned his attention to his crab. It made another cracking sound.

"Aaaah! That hurt even more! Please, don't eat me!"

Ethan slammed the crab down onto the table, half turning in his seat to glare at her even harder. "Can you not?"

"What's the matter?" she asked, widening her eyes innocently. "It's just a little joke."

Their interaction got everyone's attention and suddenly everyone stopped what they were doing to stare at her and Ethan.

Ethan

The lack of crab on Ria's plate told Ethan exactly what the problem was, and he probably would have been sympathetic if she'd just *told* him instead of mimicking tiny crab screams. She wasn't used to crab feasts. That was fine.

Making his crab pretend scream in pain and beg not to be eaten was not.

His hand was itching to pull her over his knee right here and now and show her why doing so was a bad idea. After all, she had asked him to be her Daddy Dom just a few hours ago.

Rule Number Two.

Right.

Not in front of his friends. They'd both agreed. No matter how tempting it was. Because he didn't need his friends hassling him over Ria any more than he needed his sister doing so.

"What's the joke?" Trish asked curiously, leaning forward to look past Ethan at Ria, just as Luna reached over to drop more crab meat onto Ria's plate. She really did love picking crabs even though she didn't eat them herself.

"Um..." Ria looked around at everyone and gave him a little sideways glance. He looked back at her, wanting to see how she would explain it. "Well, I might have been making Ethan's crab talk."

"Talk?" Pierce's brow furrowed in confusion.

"You know, like 'please don't eat me' and making a little screaming noise when he tried to crack its leg..." Her voice trailed off as Jillian and Caitlyn cracked up. Pierce looked horrified.

"But why?" Sebastian asked, looking down at the crab in front of him, apparently bewildered. "And why is Ethan taking it so badly?"

"You try eating a crab while someone makes little screaming noises at you," Ethan retorted.

Still cackling, Jill reached over to lift the pincer of Sebastian's crab.

"Please, don't eat me!" she squeaked in a high-pitched voice. Sebastian scowled at her.

"Yeah, see? Not so easy when it's your crab talking to you."

While Ethan was speaking, Ria picked up some of the crab on her plate and dunked it in the butter before taking a bite. "It's really good," she said enthusiastically, like she was trying to change the subject. She grimaced though as she said it, because Christian had just cracked another crab open. Not that she tried tormenting *him* with her little screams. That was being reserved specifically for Ethan, apparently.

"You should try cracking one of your own," he said, reaching over and grabbing one to put on her plate. Ria stared down at it like it was going to suddenly come to life and attack her. "I'll show you how."

He picked up another one for himself so he could start at the very beginning and show her. Once she'd done it a few times for herself, she'd get over it. Theoretically, he got it. He remembered being a kid and being both horrified and fascinated by the process. Molly had been more reluctant at first, having a similar reaction to Ria when she realized she was expected to break them open herself, but by the time she was a teenager, she picked crabs with the best of them.

"So, you place your fingers here and here and... What are you doing?"

Instead of following his directions, she'd picked up the crab by its pincers so that it was turned away from her. As he asked the question, she started making it do a little dance.

"Oh, I'm just a little crab," she sang, clearly making up the notes as she went along. "And now a giant person is going to crack my legs open and eat me..."

"That doesn't sound so bad," Caitlyn quipped with a snicker, causing another round of laughter. Giggling, Ria turned toward Ethan, making the crab do a little kick-line routine at him.

"That does it," he said, throwing down his napkin and getting to his feet. Fuck rule two.

He had Ria out of her seat and over his shoulder before she could think of something else for the crab to sing.

CHAPTER 9

RIA

Oops. Might have taken that a little too far. But she was really freaking out inside, she just didn't feel like she could show that in front of people who weren't, and so she'd tried to freak them out a little too. Now that she was over Ethan's shoulder, she could see that.

"Yeah, Ethan, show her who's boss!" Sebastian called after them, and everyone cheered. Ria lifted up her head to glare at them all, a little worried that maybe Caitlyn might not be okay with what was happening too, but Ethan's ex was clapping and laughing right along with the rest of her friends.

So that was one worry down.

Now she just needed to be concerned about what Ethan had planned.

"What about Rule Number Two?" she asked as he stomped inside.

"Fuck Rule Number Two."

Her traitorous pussy fluttered.

There was something about being carted off over a

man's shoulder like he was a caveman that just flat out did things to her libido. It was an entirely new experience, and not a particularly comfortable one, especially as all the blood rushed to her head, and yet she was still somehow enjoying herself.

It wasn't easy to see where they were, but it looked like some kind of sitting room. The door closed behind them with an ominous bang and she could see they were headed toward a big, navy couch that matched the cream-and-navy carpet he was walking across.

"Well okay then... Eek!" She found herself being moved again, and just as quickly as he'd gotten her over his shoulder, he sat down and had shifted her to over his knee.

How had he done that?

She wondered if he'd be amenable to demonstrating in slow motion later.

For research purposes.

"Um, I thought we were supposed to be talking about rules, and consequences, and limits later tonight," she said, pushing herself up to peer over her shoulder at him. The hard look she got in return, complete with blazing dark eyes, made her insides do a complicated tango.

"Oh, we will, but we're going to do a little prep discussion now." His hand came down to rest on her upturned ass, and a shiver went up her spine.

I'm gonna get spanked!

Hooray! said her pussy.

At least, that's what her pussy would be saying if it could talk. But that didn't stop her stomach from flipping over in nervous anticipation.

"I'm assuming that in your books, spankings are a

common consequence? At least, it seems like it from the Daddy Dom books I've read."

"You've read Daddy Dom books?" Color her surprised.

"I've read a few. Mostly because I wanted to know what Caitlyn and the others found so interesting about them," he admitted.

Hearing that he'd done it for his ex could have made her jealous, but really, she found it sweet. That just showed he'd been a good boyfriend in the past. At least in that way. They'd broken up for a reason. She should find out—no. Not her business. This wasn't a real relationship after all. It was just... research. Housemates with benefits. And spankings. "It's very possible I've read at least one of yours, because she really does love your books, but I'd have to ask her to know for sure."

Oh. Ria wasn't sure how she felt about that. She put a lot of her own fantasies in her books. If Ethan had read them... that made her feel vulnerable in a way she hadn't expected.

"The point is, when a little girl is being a brat, she gets spanked right?" He tapped his hand against her bottom, not nearly hard enough to be called a swat, but it was a definite threat.

"Um, well, yes, but I didn't know I was being a brat."

Ethan snorted.

"Okay, well, I didn't mean to be a brat... I just..." Her voice trailed off.

"You just what?" He shifted her on his lap and, oh hey, she really could feel his erection against her side. Ethan gave her another little tap, this one a bit harder when she didn't answer him right away.

"I'm freaking out about my food looking at me and

having to break it open by myself and pick out its insides, okay?" She dropped her head down so she didn't have to look at him anymore and also because she was getting a crick in her neck. "It's freaky! And I was uncomfortable, and I wanted to make you uncomfortable too because I was the weirdo who was freaking out while everyone else is acting like it's total normal to just break open what used to be a living creature and pull out its insides to eat!" Panting, Ria ran out of steam.

"So you were deliberately trying to make me uncomfortable and unable to eat my hard-earned lunch?"

"I didn't know it while I was doing it, I was just reacting. It wasn't deliberate. But, you know, I had a few moments to think on our way in here about why I was doing what I was doing, and that's the conclusion I came up with." Though she did feel kind of bad now. Just because she was uncomfortable didn't mean others had to be. She'd never gone hunting or anything like that though, so this was her first experience seeing a formerly alive meal reach her plate from beginning to end. But that didn't mean that Ethan shouldn't have gotten to enjoy his food.

"Sounds to me like you've earned a spanking, little girl. Do you disagree?"

"No," she said in a little voice, and he gave her butt another tap. Ow. That was a much stingier tap than before.

"How do you address me while you're being punished?"

"No, Daddy." It was easier to say this time than it had been the first time, but it turned her on just as much. Actually, literally everything about this except for thinking about how uncomfortable she'd been over the crabs was turning her on… but the crabs were becoming a distant memory while she focused on the feel of Ethan's thighs under her body, his hand cupping her butt, his cock against her side…

"Your safeword is 'red.' You can also say 'yellow' if you need me to slow down."

"Actually, my safeword is 'meatloaf,'" she told him. She *felt* him pause.

"Meatloaf?"

"You know from the song… I'll do anything, but I won't do that?" She giggled as she heard him sigh and mutter something that sounded suspiciously like 'writers.'

"Okay then, meatloaf it is. And now I'm going to demonstrate why you don't try to ruin Daddy's meals." Before she could respond, his hand came down hard on her butt.

"Ow!" That had been no little tap, not like the previous ones. That *stung*. "That hurt!"

"That's the point, little girl. Now hold still and take your punishment like a good girl." He easily caught her hands when she tried to reach back to cover her butt, pinning them in the small of her back.

Oh god… it's just like my fantasy…

But in her fantasy, the spanking hadn't hurt that much.

"Ow! Ow! Ow!" Ria squirmed on his lap with each smack of his hard hand against her bottom. That *hurt!* "Daddy, stop!"

"Isn't that what I asked you to do at the table? And you didn't, did you?"

"Noooo…" It came out as a long whine, and then she shrieked as his hand came down on a spot it had already spanked. That hurt even more!

None of it was enough to make her cry yet, but she could feel some tears coming, not so much from the pain but from realizing that she'd been kind of rude. More than kind of. Trying to ruin someone else's meal just because she was uncomfortable with hers was pretty shitty.

No wonder Ethan wanted to spank her.

She sniffled a little, and he immediately stopped the spanking, placing one hand on her backside. Ria felt him lean forward, like he was trying to look at her.

"How are you feeling, little girl?"

"Bad," she admitted. "I'm sorry I tried to ruin your lunch."

"Thank you. And don't worry, you didn't ruin it. I'm going to go back out there and finish enjoying my meal. If you'd like, you can have a hot dog like Luna."

"No, the crab really is good, I just... I don't think I can pick my own."

"That's okay, Luna will be happy to pick it for you." He chuckled as he pulled her up onto his lap. Ria squirmed as her spanked butt rested against his thigh. She knew he'd gone easier on her than any of the Doms in her books ever did, but she still felt the heat and the lingering sting.

Ethan studied her face, lifting his hand to swipe away the one tear that had fallen with his thumb.

"Are you sure you're okay?" he asked. "I know this was your first spanking."

"I'm okay, Daddy." It was getting easier to remember to call him that. Especially with her bottom still throbbing the way it was. She felt more submissive. And now that he was holding her, cradling her, she also felt taken care of. Which was exactly how she'd always imagined it would feel.

There was just one thing missing.

"Okay, well I guess we should get back to—" Ethan's suggestion was cut off as Ria placed her hands on his cheeks and leaned in to kiss him.

A rush of heat went through her, a kind of shock at her own daring, and for a moment he froze with his lips against her and she thought he was going to push her away... but then his hands tightened on her waist, his lips parting, and he returned the kiss.

Oh man, did he return the kiss.

She'd had the reins for about two-point-five seconds before he took over, *thoroughly*.

She lost control of the kiss, and what remained of anything holding back her hormones. Twisting on his lap, she ended up straddling him, their mouths still fused together, tongues dancing. The heat from her bottom was changing, the throbbing no longer at all painful, instead it was turning into a throbbing between her legs rather than across the surface of her butt.

His hands gripped her cheeks, digging in and making her whimper as she rubbed herself against the thick bulge of his erection. Her need grew along with the intensity of their kiss, her nipples hardening and aching, her pussy clenching and throbbing, and she moaned against his lips as his fingers kneaded her bottom.

Then he pulled away from the kiss and began moving his lips down her neck, one of his hands sliding up the side of her body to cup her breast.

"Oh fuck yes..." She dug her own fingers into his shoulders, shuddering at the sensations that swept through her. It had been way, way too long since she'd had a man touch her at all, much less one as good at it as Ethan. Her nerve endings felt like they were on fire.

Fingers slid into her shirt from the bottom, pushing it up, and had just reached her bra when someone knocked on the door behind them.

Ria shrieked and fell off of Ethan's lap, which made her butt throb again for the wrong reason. Twisting around she looked up to see that the door had a window on it. Ethan had taken them into a sunroom. Pierce was standing on the other side of the door, pointing at Ethan and glaring.

Up on the couch, Ethan sighed.

"I don't think Pierce wants us sullying his couch," he said, getting to his feet and holding out his hand to Ria. Blushing hotly, she took it.

"Well, if I'd known there was a window there..."

"Well, if I'd known what you were going to do, I would have warned you." Ethan pulled her flush against him for a moment, so she could feel his hard body pressing against hers.

Ria's breath caught in her throat again as her pulse went haywire and her body tried to melt.

"To be continued... later tonight."

CHAPTER 10

RIA

The worst part about the whole thing was walking back outside where everyone clearly knew what they'd been doing. It was a walk of shame that hadn't even come with an orgasm. Instead, she was squirming inside and out, and her butt felt extra sensitive.

Thankfully, no one acted like it was weird that Ethan had just caveman-hauled her off over his shoulder. They all just smiled and welcomed them back as if they'd gone to grab something from the kitchen. Though, Luna did shoot Ria a sympathetic look when she sat down and winced as her butt hit the hard wooden bench.

Ouch.

And Ethan hadn't even taken off her capris to spank her. Not that the fabric was all that thick, but right now she was very thankful for the little bit of protection it had given her.

"Here you go," Luna said cheerfully, passing a plate of crab meat across the table to Ria. It was an actual mound. She must have been picking since the moment Ethan carried Ria inside.

"Thank you." Because the crab really was good, but she didn't think she could pick it herself. She was also really glad she hadn't had to watch Luna pick the crabs. This way she hadn't seen it happen and ignorance was truly bliss. Also, she was now starving, so she dug into the crab meat and corn on the cob, listening to the conversation around her and doing her best not to be hyperaware of Ethan beside her or the tingling in her buttocks as she sat.

As she ate, it got easier to ignore the sharp cracks of the shells breaking and the way the crabs were staring at her from the middle of the table.

"So, what else do we do?" she asked. Clearly, she was going to need to include some kind of crab feast in her book, though she didn't think she'd go into too much detail about the actual crab eating, which meant she needed to know more about the rest of it.

Everyone kind of paused, and she looked around to realize they were all staring at her.

"Do?" Trish asked.

"Um, yeah, during a crab feast, what else do you guys do?"

"This is it." Sebastian swept his hand over the table, indicating the food laid out there. "It's a crab *feast*."

"Oh... so you don't play games or anything?" Sure, it was a feast, but she'd thought there'd be something more. They were going to spend the entire afternoon just... eating?

Granted, the crabs took a while to crack open and eat, but still.

Everyone looked at each other, bemused, like they were trying to figure out what else they might do.

"Sometimes we play cornhole," Jillian finally said.

Ria blinked. She couldn't have heard that correctly. But she couldn't think of what else might sound like 'cornhole' and no one else was chiming in. "I'm sorry, you play what?" she asked. "Did you say *cornhole?*"

Christian snickered. "Not that kind of cornhole."

Laughter rang out as everyone realized what kind of cornhole she was thinking of, which was reassuring. After all, she did know they were all into kink. It wasn't entirely her fault her head had started going to a weird place.

"It's like a bean-bag-toss game," Caitlyn explained, still snickering.

"But you call it *cornhole.*"

"Yup."

Well okay then. Apparently, no one else was going to acknowledge that 'cornhole' was what some people said to refer to butt holes. It didn't make sense to her, but she was starting to accept that as par for the course. Life was very different here. She couldn't imagine sitting down and eating for an entire afternoon in New York. Maybe an entire evening, at a fancy restaurant, where there would be multiple courses... but just one dish? For hours? With nothing else planned? She couldn't imagine.

Granted, there was also the dessert course, and the Smith Island cake and Berger cookies were just as good as promised. She was fascinated by the cake in particular and the tiny layers it had. How did someone even make that? When she asked, she was informed it was a secret. She'd just have to look it up on the internet later. Surely there was some information about it out there.

After stuffing themselves, Pierce did end up bringing out his cornhole set. It had six bean bags in two different colors, and two large boards with two holes in them to try and toss the bags in. They were *not* decorated with the state flag, instead they each had an angry-looking crab and a beach scene on them. Considering all the crabs they'd just eaten, Ria found the angry crab to be pretty appropriate.

It wasn't the most physical game, but it was enough that she managed to shake off some of the post-meal lethargy that had started to hit. The fact that she and Ethan were on the same team—and therefore on opposite sides of the game—meant she got to enjoy looking at him, but they couldn't do much flirting. Which wasn't the worst thing, since she was standing next to Caitlyn for the whole game, who really didn't seem to mind what was going on between them, but Ria still felt a little awkward, with Caitlyn being his ex and all.

By the time she and Ethan got in the car to head back to his house, she was feeling buzzed and energized again. She'd been hyperaware of him all afternoon, but it was even worse once they were confined to close quarters, heading to the same location. Especially since the watchful eyes of his friends were no longer on them. She couldn't decide if she was more nervous or excited.

"Did you have a good time today?" he asked, breaking the silence between them after a few minutes.

"I had an amazing time. I wasn't sure what to expect, but it was a lot of fun. Well, after I got past all the trauma."

Ethan chuckled, reaching over to put his hand atop hers on her thigh. Ria's skin tingled in response, all the little hairs on the back of her neck standing up in happy attention. She pressed her thighs together, trying not to remember what it had felt like to have his hands all over her.

Somehow, she managed to make sensible conversation until they reached his house, at which point she started feeling really awkward. How did one transition from a drive home to "take me, Daddy"?

Turned out, she didn't need to worry. As soon as they got through the front door, Ethan grabbed hold of her hand and pulled her against him.

"I have been waiting to do this all day," he murmured, just before his lips crashed against hers, claiming her in a kiss as he simultaneously kicking the door closed and pushed her up against the wall.

Oh hell yes, take me Daddy!

Ethan

The afternoon had been pure torture, spending time with Ria after spanking her but not being able to get his hands on her. Even watching her learn how to play cornhole and slowly get better at tossing the bean bags had been excruciating. The way her breasts bounced when she finally got one in the hole and started jumping up and down in celebration. The way she squirmed every time she sat down, the tenderness from the spanking he'd administered clearly lingering... as was the arousal.

Yup, he'd been waiting all afternoon to pick back up where they'd left off, and he wasn't going to let his chance pass him by.

Considering the way she enthusiastically kissed him back, wrapping her arms around his neck, he didn't have to worry about her changing her mind either. Reaching down, he grabbed hold of her butt and felt her little bounce as she realized what he was trying to do. Then she was up, her legs wrapping around his waist, his hands cupping her sweet cheeks so he could hold her against him as he pulled them away from the wall and started walking her toward the bedroom.

His cock was rock-hard already, the need to get his hands all over her driving him forward.

As he shouldered his way into his room—because there was no way he was taking her into his sister's room— he pulled away from the kiss long enough to look her in the eyes.

"Do you remember your safeword?"

"Meatloaf." She grinned back at him, her eyes sparkling. "Do you think I'm going to need it?"

"Depends on how far you want to go with me."

"I want it all, Daddy. For research purposes."

The way she said the second part was almost prim and he had to shake his head. There was that bratty side, making its way back out again, despite the spanking she'd had earlier.

The only problem he could see was not wanting to embarrass himself by coming too quickly, and he wasn't sure how much control he was going to have once he got inside her. It had been a while since his last time with anyone and he could already feel his control shredding after the long day of waiting.

"My last doctor appointment I got tested and they came back all negative. I haven't been with anyone since." He held his gaze level. "But we can still use condoms for everything, if you'd prefer. I have some flavored ones."

Ria blinked. "Same situation for me... and I'm okay with no condom for oral. I'm on birth control but..."

"Better safe than sorry. Good girl." He said it because he liked to see her reaction to the accolade, and she didn't disappoint. This close to her, he could see her pupils dilate as she sucked in a breath, her cheeks flushing pink in response.

Good. They were on the same page.

Releasing his grip on her bottom, he let her slide down his front to her knees in front of him.

"I think you still owe me a penance from earlier, little girl." Interest flared in her eyes as he undid the knot on the front of his trunks. Dammit. He was definitely going to need to wear something with a belt from here on out. Considering what she wrote, he bet she had a few specific fantasies, even if he never actually used it. "I want you to use that sassy little mouth to show Daddy how sorry you are."

His dick pulsed as she smiled up at him, her eyes lighting with aroused excitement.

Were they going from zero to sixty really fucking fast?

Hell yeah. They only had a month, after all. There was no point in holding back. Either they were going to crash and burn and spend an uncomfortable month together, or they were going to enjoy the next few weeks. So however short the time, he might as well have fun with the good part.

His dick agreed with him wholeheartedly, though the appendage was probably biased as Ria wrapped her fingers around the shaft, her pink tongue flicking out over the head. Ethan groaned, reaching down with one hand to grab hold of the ponytail that had been driving him wild.

"Open up, little girl, I want those lips wrapped around my cock. Fuck..." He groaned as she obeyed, parting her lips and taking the tip of his cock between them, her tongue laving over the sensitive tip. His hips thrust forward, sliding deeper into her mouth, savoring the wet heat that engulfed him.

It felt so fucking good.

And there she was, on her knees before him, taking Daddy's cock in her mouth like a good girl. The only thing that would have made this better was if he'd been able to do it right after her spanking, when her butt was still pink... but she probably would have been even more embarrassed had Pierce caught them in *that* act, so this was for the best.

Holding her head tightly in his grip, Ethan thrust forward, feeling her whimper vibrate along the length of his cock as more of it slid over her tongue. She sucked hard, drawing him in, and he groaned again. The way she was looking up at him as she swallowed inch after inch of his cock was making his knees weak—and he'd already been riding the edge of his arousal.

"That's it, good girl. Take Daddy's cock down your throat."

Fuck him if she didn't follow direction. Ethan's knees really did almost buckle as she hummed along his length and pushed down, the tip of his cock bumping against the back of her throat and then continuing onward, as if she didn't have a gag reflex.

"Fuck!" He shuddered, feeling her throat muscles working to swallow him, closing his eyes to savor the sensations traveling over his cock. He could feel his balls tightening as his need rose higher.

Ria pulled back and then plunged back down again, her lips pressing against his groin as she swallowed him, before she slid away to breathe. It was the best head he'd ever gotten, her enthusiasm taking it from a normal blow job to cock worshiping as she did her best to swallow him whole. Even the delicate scrape of her teeth along his shaft increased his pleasure. Her hands braced against his thighs, fingers digging in as she bobbed her head up and down on his cock.

He might have her hair in his fingers, but she had him by the balls and she was doing her best to give him everything he'd asked for.

"Oh fuck... I'm going to come..." He gave her the heads-up, just in case she wanted to pull away, but his words made her redouble her efforts. "Fuck!"

Ethan thrust forward as he hit his peak, sliding in deep to pour his release down her throat. She sucked, her fingers digging into the backs of his thighs to hold him in place as she swallowed every last drop.

Panting, he held himself in place, shuddering through the last spasms of his release before he eased back, relaxing his grip on her ponytail. He met her gaze, his own softening as he looked down at her.

"Very good girl." He held out his hand for her to take, helping her to stand, before turning, sweeping her off her feet and tossing her onto the bed as she squealed. "My turn."

CHAPTER 11

Holy fuck. She could taste Ethan on her tongue as he crawled onto the bed with her, completely shucking off the rest of his clothing as he did so. Ria licked her lips, not just because there was a drop of cum still on them, but because he just looked so damn good.

Ethan was lickable.

And she'd thoroughly enjoyed licking him. And sucking him. She'd really, really enjoyed the look on his face when she was able to swallow him whole. It was mostly luck that she'd never had much of a gag reflex anyway, and once she realized what it meant for a blow job, she'd practiced till she was perfect. Because she was a pleaser at heart and being able to see *that look* on a man's face, and know that she was the one who had put it there, was ridiculously satisfying.

Seeing it on Ethan's had been even more so, because he definitely hadn't expected it.

Being called 'good girl' for it?

Heaven.

"You are fucking amazing," he murmured as he leaned over her, his hands going to her shirt and tugging it upwards. Ria arched on the bed, moving to help him get it off... as soon as it was over her head, he used it to pin down her arms, lowering his lips to get a kiss.

It wasn't bondage, exactly, but it completely immobilized her upper body, and the heat that flared in her core in response was shocking. She'd never had anyone hold her down, and she'd never considered that her clothing might be used against her in such a manner. Heat and need flushed through her, pebbling her nipples, and making her clench. She wrapped her legs around him, feeling his hard body against hers. He might have just gotten off, but that didn't stop him from kissing her deeply, his free hand running down her arm to her breasts and cupping one through her bra.

For the first time, Ria cursed the thin padding of the cup. It was great for making sure her nipples didn't poke through her shirt, and absolute shit for letting her feel Ethan's touch. Right now, she wished she'd worn one of her bras that didn't have the padding, because she wanted to feel him...

A moment later she got her wish as he shifted atop her, his hand moving so he could slip his fingers into the top of her bra and cup her breast. Ria moaned against his lips as she felt the warmth of his hand curving over the soft mound, his thumb rubbing against her nipple.

The blow job might have been fast and furious, but now Ethan was taking his time. He'd gotten his edge off, but Ria was still squirming in need. Her orgasm was still waiting, and the more he touched her, the worse her need got... The fact that she couldn't even touch him back right now, that she was helplessly pinned beneath him, was sending her arousal out of control.

Even when he kept going, releasing her arms from their impromptu bondage so that he could take off her bra completely, he kept teasing her rather than giving her what she so badly needed. He devoured her breasts, licking and suckling on her nipples until she was begging him for more. The tiny buds throbbed as he nipped at them, teasing the sensitive nubs, tormenting her with his mouth.

By the time he stripped off her capris and panties, she was soaking wet, squirming with need... and when he lowered his mouth between her legs, it was all she could do not to howl with pleasure from the erotic contact. He teased her there too, with her fingers holding onto his hair, trying to pull him more firmly against her swollen folds. He licked and nibbled, and thoroughly avoided the spot where she most wanted contact.

Ria moaned, writhing in place, as he wrapped his arms around her, his broad shoulders pushing her legs back, his hands prying them farther apart, so she was unable to stop his merciless assault.

"Please, Daddy... I need... I need..." She sobbed as he flicked his tongue over her clit, giving her the tiniest bit of what her throbbing body demanded, while still leaving her unfulfilled. She needed to come so badly that she ached with it, and yet some part of her loved that he continued to deny her.

"Were you a naughty girl today?" he asked, his voice a low croon, before he slid his tongue through her folds again.

Ria moaned, writhing in place as he tormented her with his oral expertise. "Yes, Daddy, I was naughty, I'm sorry!" She truly was too. She'd rather have another spanking than more of this.

"And are you ever going to interrupt Daddy's meal again?"

"Nooooo..." The word became elongated when he sucked her clit into his mouth—just for a moment. Just long enough to make her body buck beneath him, only for her to find that he had her completely pinned down. Her pussy was wide open to him, completely vulnerable, and he was taking advantage of it. "Daddy, please!"

"Shh, princess, Daddy's enjoying his meal. No interrupting, remember?"

And with that, Ethan went right back to his business, stoking her fires higher and higher with every flick of his tongue. Ria's toes curled, and she panted for breath, tugging on his hair so fiercely that she was almost surprised it didn't come out in her hands.

"Daddy, pleaaaaaa—" Ria's plea turned into a scream of passion as Daddy's mouth moved to her clit again, finally sucking the swollen, aching nub between his lips and keeping it there. Ecstasy slammed into her with a force that was almost painful, and her body tried to levitate off the bed in response.

Waves of pleasure rolled over her, swamping her, as the delayed release finally exploded, as if holding back for so long had made the inevitable all the more intense. He kept his mouth on her, suckling and flicking his tongue against the tender bud, sending her through paroxysms of hot bliss that grew in intensity. Just when she thought she couldn't take anything more, he released her, and she went limp on the bed, panting for breath, her entire body buzzing from the erotic high.

She was so inwardly focused, she didn't hear the

tearing of the condom wrapper, and had almost forgotten there would be *more* until Ethan was looming over her.

"Daddy, wait!" She pressed her hands against his chest as the tip of his cock slid against her swollen, sensitive folds.

Ethan paused, looking down at her, one eyebrow rising.

"It's too much... I can't take it..."

"Yes, you can, princess. You're going to take Daddy's cock and you're going to love it." His words made her insides clench, and as he took her hands from his chest and pinned them down on either side of her head just as he thrust into her, Ria felt like her entire body was about to float away. The slick glide of his cock into her, stretching her open, pushing deep inside her, when she was already overstimulated, still quivering from the incredible orgasm... None of her exes had ever done anything like this.

None of them had feasted on her until she was practically dizzy from the ecstasy. None of them had pushed her. None of them had pinned her down and had their way with her. None of them had called her princess while treating her like their own personal fuck toy.

It was like all her fantasies had come to life at once, funneled into one man, who was currently fucking her into sexual oblivion.

Ria cried out, writhing underneath Ethan as he pounded into her, her legs wrapping around him and trying to hold him in place against her. All that did was make his strokes shorter, harder, his body rubbing against her clit and sending another wave of shocking ecstasy through her. She could feel literal tears sliding down the sides of her face as the overstimulation drove her body to the brink...

"Come for me one last time, princess. Come all over Daddy's cock."

The final barrier broke loose and Ria's entire body spasmed as the most intense orgasm she'd ever experienced exploded inside her, and her pussy clamped down on his cock as he thrust in hard.

Ethan

Holy fuck.

Ria was coming apart beneath him and it was the most fucking beautiful thing he'd ever seen. He could feel her body undulating against his, the sweet grip of her pussy spasming around his cock, and he groaned as he thrust in hard, rubbing his body against her pussy and making her scream for him again.

Fuck yes.

The tight clamp of her muscles rippling with pleasure as they massaged his length gave him all he needed reach his own culmination. He shuddered against her, her pussy clenching and milking him as he filled the condom with his second orgasm of the evening.

"Fuck..." He braced himself against his forearms so he didn't completely collapse on top of her.

As over sensitized as he knew she must be right now, he was feeling the same. His skin was practically humming from the intensity of his orgasm... his *two* orgasms. No wonder his nerve endings were overwhelmed.

"Fuck..." Ria repeated after him. She yawned, her eyelashes fluttering. "I can't feel my legs."

Ethan preened, taking that as a compliment. Because it was. Damn right she couldn't feel her legs. The urge to lean down and brush a kiss over her lips was strong, but he resisted. This was... research. A month-long arrangement. They weren't dating, they weren't boyfriend and girlfriend, and he wanted to make sure neither of them got confused about that.

"I'm going to go clean up," he said, pulling away from her.

"Mmm." Ria yawned again, closing her eyes.

He liked seeing her in his bed a little too much.

Going to the bathroom, Ethan took care of the condom and cleaned up before also making a pit stop in the kitchen for two glasses of water and a candy bar, just in case she needed something. But when he got back, she was completely passed out, her hair spread across his pillowcase—not quite snoring but breathing loudly enough that it was audible.

Damn. She was really cute when she slept.

So much for aftercare though.

It had been a long day; he shouldn't be too surprised.

The only question was whether or not he should wake her up and send her back to her own room. No, he wouldn't need to wake her. That would be rude. He could just carry her and take her back to her own bed. Because sex was one thing, but sleeping together...

That was the kind of intimacy that could get confusing if they were keeping things casual. Since they were living together, he should probably put as many boundaries in place as he could.

But she looked so damn cute. And comfortable.

Ethan found himself crawling into bed beside her rather than taking her out of it. This wasn't the normal casual relationship after all. There was a hard expiration date of when she'd be going back to her own home, which was several states away. So it probably wouldn't really matter whether he let her sleep in his bed a few times or not. And it was only the first night. He didn't have to do this every time. Heck, she probably wouldn't fall right to sleep every time.

So, no big deal.

That's what he kept telling himself as he snuggled up behind her, wrapping his arm over her body and letting his limp cock press against her bottom. Damn, he wished he could still feel the heat from her spanking.

Closing his eyes, he slipped off to sleep with an ease he hadn't expected.

CHAPTER 12

<u>RIA</u>

When Ethan made a promise to help with research, he *meant* it.

After their first night together, she hadn't fallen asleep in his room again, but that hardly mattered. She'd woken up wrapped up in his arms, her eyelashes feeling oddly crusty, and realized she'd fallen asleep in full makeup. Thankfully, she'd been able to sneak out and take care of her face and hair before he'd woken up.

Men! She couldn't believe she'd slept the whole night without cleaning her face off, and she'd made him promise not to let her do that again—which he'd only agreed to after a rather epic five-minute rant about the bugs that started showing up on unremoved makeup. Blech. Ria loved her makeup. She did not like bugs, not even microscopic ones.

After showing him a few pictures online and making him read the article, he'd agreed that he'd never let her fall asleep with full makeup on again. And then chuckled at her sugary sweet 'thank you, Daddy' response.

They both still had to work during the day, but since then they'd spent every evening together and she'd spent every night getting railed by Daddy's cock. One time was during lunch when she'd been at the house rather than the coffee shop, where he'd laid her out on the kitchen island and eaten pussy for his meal before flipping her over and plowing into her from behind, while pinning her down to the cold surface.

He hadn't even bothered taking off any of her clothes other than her panties.

Of course, she'd worn a skirt that day, open for something exactly like that, but she hadn't expected it in the middle of the day.

Her pussy was starting to get sore... and yet she enjoyed that as well.

The only thing that hadn't happened was that she hadn't gotten another spanking yet. Part of the problem was that while she had no problem being sassy, she didn't actually like being *bad*. And Ethan apparently found her sass cute. And hot. He was perfectly willing to put her on her knees and fill her sassy mouth with cock to shut her up—which gave her poor pussy a needed break—but so far, he hadn't spanked her butt again.

Ria hadn't been able to make herself misbehave to get what she wanted either.

Finally, the perfect opportunity to push him a little presented itself when they were going away to Ocean City for the weekend. Christian had offered up his beach condo to them. The weather was going to be gorgeous, though a little cool for the beach, but Ria was happy to take high seventies since it was the warmest weekend in May so far.

However, Ethan had been up late the night before

working on something—after fucking her senseless—and then up again early this morning to keep working so they could leave Thursday night and have all day Friday there. One look at him with his reddened eyes and the way he kept yawning told her that he should not be driving, even though he said he was fine.

"Absolutely not," she said firmly, crossing her arms over her chest and standing in his way so he couldn't open the trunk of his car. "We're taking my car."

"No, we're taking my car." He yawned again. "I'm driving. You don't know the way."

"No, you're not." Yup, this was an easy situation to push back, because she was also right. "You're exhausted. You're so tired you can barely keep your eyes open. It's just going to keep getting later and darker, and you are in no position to be driving for hours. I'm driving, we're taking my car, and I can use the GPS just like every other person who's going somewhere they've never been before."

His shoulders went back, chest puffing up, and a little thrill went through her... right before he suddenly sighed and all the tension in him went out. "Fine. You drive. I'll take a little nap and then we'll switch before the Bay Bridge."

"Fine."

His capitulation was both a relief—because she really didn't think he should be the one driving—and a little disappointing—because she really did want a spanking.

It did show good judgment on his part, as well as respect for her, which was way better than if he'd ignored her. That he could admit when she was right made her like him even more.

Maybe she'd find a way to earn a spanking over the

weekend. They were going to be spending the entire time together, instead of just evenings. Something would surely come up.

They got on the road, swinging into a gas station to fill up and grab snacks. They'd already had dinner, but Ethan insisted on getting road-trip snacks and that didn't sound like a terrible idea to Ria. Not that he got a chance to eat them. Five minutes after they left the gas station, he was passed out. As evidenced by his snoring, which must have been from his position because he hadn't snored that night she'd slept in his room. At least, not that she'd noticed.

Shaking her head in amusement, she turned down the music so it wouldn't wake him and kept on driving. It was getting dark when she started seeing the signs for the Bay Bridge coming up. Cruising along in the left lane, she glanced over at the still-sleeping Ethan, and decided she didn't need to wake him up. She flipped on the car lights and ignored the signs warning that the last exit was coming up.

She'd seen people talking on social media about how scary the bridge was, but she was from New York. Bridges were bridges, and there were plenty of them around her that freaked people out too.

Humming along with the music, she went through the toll booth. Before they left, Ethan had insisted on putting his EZ pass on the inside of her windshield, so she didn't need to worry about the toll charges.

"Nice and easy," she said smugly, glancing over at him again before returning her gaze to the roadway. It was a lot darker now, but she could see a large bridge looming ahead, lit against the night sky. There were two of them, actually, one on the right and one on the left, the traffic going back and forth across the Bay.

Some traffic cones directed her more to the left, and she followed them, watching the lights of some of the other cars behind her moving to the right. Okay well that was weird. The cones were pushing her further left, rather than bringing her back to the right side of the bridge and—

"Oh my God!" she screeched as she saw lights coming right at her. It took her a moment to realize that they weren't coming *right* at her. They were coming from the lane next to the one she was in, but somehow, she was getting onto the wrong bridge! She was going on the bridge on the left, not the right!

"What? What's happening?" Ethan bolted upright, at least he tried to, before his seatbelt caught him and snapped him back down into the seat. "Ria, what's wrong?"

"I'm on the wrong side of the bridge!" she screeched, just as honking came from behind her. Bright lights flashed in the rearview mirror. She wasn't the only one on the wrong side either! Someone was behind her, and they were honking at her for some reason. What the hell was she supposed to do?

Ethan managed to sit up and immediately started laughing.

"Drive Ria, you're in the reversible lane."

"The what?" But between his order to drive, and the car honking behind her, she put her foot on the gas pedal despite the way she was shaking. More lights were coming toward her and the edge of the bridge was *so close* to the right side of her car, but she definitely couldn't move to the left with cars actually coming *at* her. Her heart was pounding so hard it was a miracle she could even hear Ethan over its thumping. Her chest constricted, making it impossible to breathe.

"The reversible lane." Ethan put his seat up, shaking his head. "It changes direction depending on the flow of traffic."

"Why the hell would they have it going in the *wrong* direction at *night?*" she asked, grimacing as the car behind her blared its horn again even though she was no longer stopped and blocking their way.

"You're going under the speed limit," Ethan said, rather than answering her question.

Pressing her lips together, Ria reluctantly started to speed up a tiny bit, so that she was at least going to the speed limit, which still felt way too fast in the dark with cars coming at her... and how was this bridge so freaking long? They were so high up and in the growing dark it looked like a terrifyingly long drop to the black water below.

"And if you'd woken me up the way I'd told you to," Ethan continued, "we wouldn't be in this lane and you wouldn't have to be the one driving across the bridge."

If she didn't need both her hands tightly gripping the steering wheel right now, she'd be tempted to punch him. There was no way she was letting go though. She swore she could feel the bridge swaying in the wind. This could not be safe. "I can't believe this is normal for you."

Ethan chuckled. "It's definitely more disturbing at night. I remember the first time I drove across after dark on this side, and I'm used to driving across this bridge. It's scary, but you've got it." He reached across and put a reassuring hand on her thigh and, damn him, it did ease some of her nervous tension. "You're doing great."

It was crazy how he was managing to actually soothe her shattered nerves, but he did.

She still didn't take a true deep breath until she was finally on the other side of the bridge, back on the right side of the highway. The car that had been behind her the entire way across the bridge blared its horn at her again as it sped around her. And she'd thought New Yorkers had tempers on the road. She was pretty sure the driver had flipped her off too.

"Good. We made it across. Now what the hell were you thinking and why didn't you wake me up?"

Ethan

Now that they were over the bridge and past the panic point, he didn't feel so bad about raising his voice, his hand gripping her thigh where he'd originally put it to help calm her.

His palm itched, as it had multiple times over the past week when Ria had gotten sassy with him. He knew she was looking for a spanking and he'd been waiting to see what she would do next before administering one, but he truly hadn't thought she'd disobey a direct order. She'd mentioned the Bay Bridge several times during conversations, so he'd figured she had some idea of what she was getting into—though unexpectedly being in the reversible lane would unnerve most people.

"I didn't think it would be that big a deal!" Ria protested. He noticed she hadn't let go of her white-knuckled grip on the steering wheel. Whatever she'd thought before, she now knew she was wrong.

"Do you still feel that way?" He shook his head. "You

know, people can *hire* someone to take them over the damn bridge. That's how much people hate driving it. Next time, *wake me up!*"

She grumbled something under her breath. He gave her another moment to answer before deciding that grumble must be all he was going to get.

"Well, while you're thinking about why you should have listened to me during the rest of the drive, you can also think about the spanking you're going to be receiving when we get there." Hiding his smile, he reclined his seat back down, crossing his arms over his chest. Even though he couldn't see her, he could feel her looking at him, and when he peeked to see what she was doing, he could see her squirming in her seat.

The anticipation of the spanking was just as much a punishment as the spanking itself. Though, the real punishment had been driving in the reversible lane in the dark, which was far worse than anything he could do to her, but he wasn't going to tell her that. She'd been bratty all week, presumably hoping to get a hand applied to her bottom.

When they got to the beach condo, he was going to give her what she'd been asking for.

CHAPTER 13

Announcing that she was getting a spanking right after they got off the bridge, when she still hadn't fully recovered, was just sadistic. Ria sent several nasty glares at Ethan—as much as she dared to take her eyes off the road. Not that he seemed to notice. She was squirming in her seat the entire rest of the way to the beach, while he apparently snoozed beside her.

The big jerk.

He finally opened his eyes and sat up when they were about ten minutes away.

"Oh wow..." Ria said as they went across another—much smaller—bridge. She could see a whole strip of land to the right and left, lit up with lights and then darkness just past them. The huge water tower announced what she already knew: they'd reached Ocean City.

"Yeah, it looks nice like this, huh?" Ethan reached over to rest his hand on her thigh again, which of course reminded her that she was going to be over his knee soon, with his hand doing much more interesting things.

Just when she'd finally gotten her mind off the subject too.

"I guess you're not going to get the chance to eat your road-trip snacks," she said, amused. Not unless he was going to tear the bag open in the next few minutes.

"That's okay, they turn into beach snacks easily."

Ria could only shake her head, because his friends had provided them with a long list of places she was supposed to get food from. She thought it was likely the snacks would come back home with them uneaten after the weekend, considering how many things she was supposed to try while she was out here. From what she could tell, a big part of Maryland culture revolved around food. Which... okay, she couldn't really complain. She was already addicted to Berger cookies and planning on buying them in bulk to take back home with her. She had plenty of room in her freezer in New York, she could stuff it full of Berger cookies to last until her next visit.

The closer they got to the condo, the antsier she got. The GPS estimated time of arrival had turned into a countdown to her spanking timer. She wasn't a fan.

Though, walking into the condo for the first time almost made her forget. The front door opened into the main room and kitchen, which had a fantastic view of the beach. Even though it was dark outside, as soon as the light was on, the interior felt both cozy and bright, thanks to all the white shiplap and light blue and yellow décor.

What made her stare were all the lighthouses.

They were *everywhere.*

The kitchen counter and the dining table and coffee tables were mostly clear, though they each had one in the middle of them, but there were no other empty flat surfaces. It wasn't just miniatures either. There were lighthouse photos and paintings on the walls, lighthouses decorating the kitchen towels, lighthouses covering the curtains at the back of the main room, which she assumed led out to a balcony... there was even a lighthouse pillow on the couch.

"Does Christian have a lighthouse fetish or something?" Ria asked, walking in slowly, taking the opportunity to look around as she did so. Ethan chuckled and came up behind her, taking her bag from her.

"He mentioned once that he liked them a lot and had a small collection, and then everyone started giving him lighthouses and his collection grew quickly. It became something of a joke, and so he just kept getting them. When he got the beach condo, he put them all here. Sometimes, when one of us stays, we'll add one and put it out without telling him and see how long it takes him to notice." Ethan's voice changed as he spoke and she looked to see him heading into a now-lit-up bedroom. Dropping his bag on the ground, he stretched, rolling his shoulders back as he turned to her and crooked his finger. "Okay princess. Enough about lighthouses. Come here."

Excitement and apprehension shivered through her. '*A spanking! Finally!*' said one half of her brain. '*A spanking! Run!*' said the other.

Running might be even more exciting but she was pretty sure it wasn't going to get her out of the spanking and, besides, she didn't want to add to her punishment. Right now, Ethan didn't seem too upset, and she didn't want him to get there. Licking her lips, she followed him into the bedroom. It was also full of lighthouses, including the sheets.

Ethan sat down on top of the lighthouse-covered

comforter and patted his knee as Ria dropped her bag beside his. "Right here, princess."

Geez, no preamble or anything, just over his knee, huh? And yet... she didn't really need a warm-up. The whole ride here had been one long, torturous wait, and she felt a sense of relief that the wait was finally over as she put herself across his lap.

Moving his legs, Ethan shifted her forward more, and Ria let out a little eep, reaching down to press her hands against the floor to help keep her balance. Her butt felt higher in the air than it had a moment ago.

"Good girl."

He flipped up her skirt as he said the words, and another little shiver went down her spine. This was already different from the previous spanking he'd given her, if only because she already felt more vulnerable. There was something about being helpless across his lap, her hands keeping her balance and unable to cover her butt, and feeling that skirt flip up to bare her bottom that made her feel wildly submissive.

Staring at the carpet—which was a pretty sandy beige color and didn't have any lighthouses on it—Ria's breath hitched as a finger hooked into her panties and slowly drew them down over her butt. Her insides clenched. It wasn't like Ethan hadn't seen her backside multiple times over the past week, but it hadn't been like *this*.

"Now, the next time I give you a direct order like, 'wake me up before the bridge,' are you going to listen?" he asked, rubbing his hand over her ass like he was warming up her skin. Which, she realized, he probably was.

"Yes, Daddy." Probably. She wasn't sure how well she would do with that long term, but she was only here for a few more weeks—a thought that made her sad so she pushed it away.

"I'm so glad to hear that," he said dryly. She tried to peek over her shoulder at him, but her current position made it difficult. The bed was higher than the couch at Pierce's had been and her head was farther down than it had been then. Plus, the side of the bed got in the way. "But there's still the matter of consequences for ignoring me today."

"Sorry Da-AH!" His hand came down sharp and swift on her butt, right in the middle of her apology— which really was sincere, even though it was more so from how harrowing the drive over the bridge had been than for disobeying. "Ow!"

His hand came down again and again as Ria squirmed on his lap, her feet kicking up a little with each impact of his palm.

Did a spanking hurt more on a bare butt? The other one had been so long ago that she couldn't really remember. It felt like this hurt more... or her memory had dimmed the pain of the previous spanking. It might just be that she felt more vulnerable without even a thin layer of cloth to provide some nominal protection.

"Oh, you're definitely going to be sorry, princess," he said sternly, hooking one hand around her hip while the other continued to apply firm discipline to her backside.

"Ow! I am, I am!" That was really starting to hurt! The crisp swats stung every time they landed on fresh skin, and even more when his hand overlapped a spot he'd smacked before. "I promise, I'll listen!"

Tears sparked in her eyes as he continued, but that didn't stop her moan when his hand dipped down between her legs to check her pussy. She was wet. Not only that, but her clit throbbed when he stroked his fingers over it. Chuckling after that discovery, Ethan went right back to spanking her while ignoring her protests. Yet she didn't say her safe word.

The heat was growing in her backside, in more than one way. Finally, Ethan pulled her up, pausing only to drag her dress up over her head before bending her over the edge of the bed. It felt like her butt was on fire, now pointing directly at him, and then she felt her bra release... and then his hand came down on her ass again.

"Daddy!"

"Just had to get one last swat in, sweetheart," he said. She heard the sound of a condom being opened and then Daddy's cock was pressing into her from behind as his hands slid underneath her body to cup her breasts. Ria moaned, lifting her hips and pushing back to take his dick deeper, pushing up onto her elbows so he could have easier access to her breasts.

He thrust in hard and deep, his hands gripping her breasts to pull her back against him, and Ria cried out as his body smacked against her sensitized ass. Her nipples throbbed in time with the clenching of her pussy as she clamped down around him, already so turned on she thought she might explode.

Ethan

Ria was fucking perfection, her reddened, heart-shaped ass warming his groin as he impaled her on his cock and held himself there to enjoy the feeling of being fully embedded inside her while the heat from her spanked bottom emanated against his skin.

"Such a good girl, taking Daddy's cock so well," he growled, bending forward, sliding his hands down on her breasts enough that he could pinch her nipples between his fingers.

Ria moaned, tossing her head back, shuddering as her pussy spasmed around him. "Oh Daddy... please..." she begged, squirming for an entirely different reason than when she'd been over his knee.

"I like it when you beg, princess," he murmured, pinching her nipples harder before dragging his cock back and thrusting in again. The warmth of her bottom heated his stomach as he started to fuck her, deliberately moving fast and hard enough that he slapped against her punished bottom with every thrust. The flesh jiggled and she cried out every time, panting for breath as he rode her from behind.

Her cries grew higher, wilder, as he moved. Despite her elbows braced against the bed, she couldn't hold herself up and she eventually dropped, trapping his hands between her and the bed. Not that he minded.

"Daddy... Daddy... I'm gonna come..."

"That's it, princess. Come for Daddy. Come all over Daddy's cock." As usual, just hearing the words set her off with a high cry that gave him such deep satisfaction.

He couldn't fucking get enough of her, which was why they'd had sex in just about every position, on every available surface in his home. The moment he talked about her being a good girl for Daddy or coming for Daddy, she turned into the most submissive little babygirl, creaming herself for him just like he'd told her to.

"Daddy!" She screamed out as Ethan railed her, fucking her through the waves of her orgasm as she started writhing beneath him, her pussy clamping down on him like she was trying to hold him in place. But he fucked her harder and harder, ignoring her cries of agonized ecstasy as his own climax neared.

Pulling back, he released her breasts, so he could stand straight and grip her hips in his hands, pinning her to the bed. Now when he looked down, he could see his cock, slick with her juices, pumping in and out of her swollen pussy, her reddened ass bouncing above it with every stroke.

Fuck.

Ethan cried out as his balls tightened, his own release rushing forward, and he buried himself inside her, letting her clenching muscles milk him of every last drop until the condom was full.

Fucking perfection.

CHAPTER 14

ETHAN

"Oh my god, it's a horse! A real horse, just wandering around!"

Taking Ria to Assateague had been a brilliant idea, especially because the water there was kinder than the waves that were pummeling the shore outside Christian's condo. They were wearing their bathing suits, though both of them kept their shirts on while they waded into the water and took a walk down the long beach. Ethan chuckled, giving her hand a squeeze.

"Did you think I was kidding?" he asked. Assateague was known for its wild horses, which roamed the island as they wished. They were far too early in the season for the swim between Assateague and Chincoteague, but that was good. The crowds at that time always kept him away.

"Hey, you were the one who said we might not see them," she countered accusingly, though she didn't sound very upset. "Do you think we can get closer?"

"Do you want me to turn you over my knee right here

on this beach?" It wasn't deserted, but if she was going to put herself in danger like that, he'd give her a swat or two. Considering the wet spray of the waves was making its way up the backs of their thighs, he might aim for that area—damp from the water, it would hurt even more. Plus, swatting her thighs wouldn't get them as much attention as if he actually spanked her. "They're still wild animals. Did you not read the website?"

He'd made sure to have her look at it on their way to the island. Sadly, the rules all had to be there for people who saw a wild horse and thought they could treat them as a riding horse. Though any horse should be treated with caution, but people could be incredibly stupid around animals, domestic and wild. On Assateague it could be even more dangerous because tourists who didn't follow the rules, or thought they were above them, sometimes fed the horses who could become incredibly aggressive in their pursuit of more food. And even if the horses weren't looking for food, they didn't necessarily like being approached by strangers. Getting too close was an all-around bad idea.

Ria sighed heavily, looking at the horse longingly.

"I know, I know... okay, just a picture then." They managed to line up a photo of her with the horse in the background so that both were easily visible. Ethan couldn't help but smile as he took it. She looked so happy.

Hell, this whole weekend she'd been bouncing—even when she wasn't bouncing on his cock. Today was all about showing her something other than the local food, and he'd packed them a picnic lunch which was waiting for them in the car. They'd already hit the important spots on the Ocean City boardwalk the night before—Thrasher's fries, Dumser's ice cream, and they would stop for some Fisher's popcorn on the way back to the condo.

Showing her around was fun, and a little dangerous. With all the time they were spending together, it was feeling a bit like a real relationship... but the clock was ticking because every day was another day closer to her return home. He really needed to keep that in mind, because he was becoming a little too comfortable with having her around.

That didn't stop him from taking her hand again once he'd gotten the picture. Or from holding it all the way home on Sunday in the car. Even when she complained about Royal Farms after they made a pit stop for gas and some snacks.

"I don't understand."

"What?"

"You call it RoFo."

"Yes."

"But 'Farms' doesn't have an 'o' in it!"

Ethan shrugged. "Why does that matter?"

"It just does! It makes no sense!"

He shrugged again. It probably didn't but he'd never really thought about it. People called Royal Farms 'RoFo' and they all knew what it meant, so did it matter that there was no 'o' in 'farms'?

Apparently, it did to Ria. She muttered about it the whole way home, though he did get her to admit that RoFo ice was indeed superior ice even if she had an issue with their name. Once they got in the door, he put her on her knees and shut her up with his favorite method. It was a nice way to end the trip.

On Monday it was back to their new schedule of work, sex, and watching tv together in the evening. Sometimes she'd read while he played video games or watched a show she wasn't interested in. It was insanely domestic. For all he'd thought she was high-maintenance when he first met her, he was coming to realize that she maintained herself. She liked pretty things and had a certain style, but she didn't require anything from him for it—though she enjoyed his appreciation.

She fit in with his friends, who all adored her. His ex clearly wanted to be her best friend. Strangely, it didn't feel awkward to hang out with Ria and Caitlyn at the same time. She fell into place like she was always supposed to be there.

That was really messing with his head. As was the fact that he didn't even bother trying to get her to move back to Molly's room at night. He liked sleeping next to her too much.

And while part of him kept warning himself against getting used to it, the other part figured he might as well enjoy it while he could. That was the part that kept winning. He wanted as much of her as he could get while she was here... and he wanted to do things with her that he hadn't with anyone else. Things he'd only fantasized about before.

Which was how she ended up over his knee before the Oriole's game they were meeting everyone at.

"I'm supposed to go to the game with a plug in my butt?" she whined as he pressed the lubricated tip to her virgin hole. Whether or not he'd ever get his cock in the tight orifice, he wasn't sure, but he knew he wanted to play with it. The first time he'd put his finger there while eating her out, she'd nearly kicked him in the head from surprise—so he'd tied her in place and continued doing what he was doing, but it had made the area much more tantalizing a target.

"That's right." He pushed in slightly, feeling the resistance, enjoying the little noise of surprise and uncertainty that she made. "It'll help remind you to be a good girl while we're out in public. Plus, it will be fun."

"I think you and I have very different ideas of fun," she grumbled, making Ethan laugh. He pushed the plug in deeper and Ria squealed.

"I think your problem is that we have exactly the same idea of what constitutes 'fun' and sometimes you wish we didn't."

Ria

Daddy hit a little too close to home with that observation. Fortunately, he didn't seem to expect a response as he pulled the plug back a bit before pushing it in deeper still and making her moan and wriggle as her backside was invaded. Ria had written about plugs and butt stuff plenty of times, but this first experience... it was more invasive, more humiliating, and more arousing than she'd imagined.

Her pussy fluttered as it pushed in, opening her up, stretching her entrance with a raw sensation as the toy rubbed against her nerve endings, causing a fluttering that was indescribable. It felt so wrong and so good at the same time. Her brain was insisting it was an 'out' hole, and yet her pussy clenched at the sensation of being filled there. Or maybe it was the idea of taking his cock there, because of course she was now wildly curious as to what *that* would feel like.

How much it would hurt.

How good it would feel.

"Ow!" She squealed as the thickest part pushed past her tight ring. She could actually feel her entrance snap into place around the little neck between the bulb and the flat base.

"Good girl," Daddy crooned, twisting it inside her.

The amount of lube meant it spun easily, despite the way her muscles clamped down around it, which was the oddest sensation. Ria moaned, shuddering a little.

"You look very pretty with a plug in your ass, princess."

"Thanks, Daddy," she replied, only a tad sarcastically, earning herself a sharp swat on her butt, right where he'd just inserted the plug, jolting it inside her. "Ow!"

Chuckling, he helped her back onto her feet, his gaze locked on her face, watching her expressions change as she adjusted to having something filling the wrong hole. The sensations between over his knee and standing were very different. Her muscles clenched, trying to hold it in, as the fear that it would fall out became very real.

That would be so embarrassing.

Maybe she should put that in a book.

Sometimes she felt sorry for what she put her heroines through... but not sorry enough to stop doing it.

"How do you feel, princess?" he asked, helping her by pulling her underwear and capris up. It felt odd being dressed, and yet she appreciated it too, because she wasn't sure how she would have bent to grab hold of her capris.

There was also something intimate about *being* dressed, even though they both knew she was fully capable of doing it herself. Maybe *because* they both knew she was capable, and yet he was doing it anyway. A kind of subtle domination over her. Maybe it wasn't that subtle. But it felt... nice. Like she was being taken care of in a way that she hadn't ever experienced in a romantic relationship before.

Sure, she was an independent woman who could do whatever she needed on her own, but it was nice that she didn't have to. And he didn't respect her less for it or think she was taking advantage of him in any way—he just wanted to take care of her and so he was.

When she got back to New York, the bar for her next boyfriend was going to be so much higher than before...

But thinking about going home made her feel sad, so she pushed that away as Daddy straightened up and smiled down at her.

"So? How do you feel?" he asked again, and she realized she'd been so lost in thought that she hadn't answered his question.

"Um... full. Very full." So full. Probably because there was something filling her that wasn't normally there. Good grief, she was supposed to be better with words than this, but it was the only description she could think of that really fit. There was no other word for it.

"Good." He appeared very pleased as he patted her on the butt. "This will help you to remember to be a good girl while we're at the game... and when we get home, you'll feel even more full when Daddy fucks you with the plug still in."

If she was going to make any protest, it would have been lost in the kiss that claimed her lips. Normally, she would say that anyone talking in third person was a douche move, but when he did it while referring to himself as Daddy... it turned both of them on.

She was starting to think of him as 'Daddy' more too,

at least in the middle of sexy times. The rest of the time he was Ethan, but now when he put his hands or lips on her, it was like a flip switched in her head and he went from Ethan to Daddy in the blink of an eye. It was hot.

Pulling away, Ethan grinned down at her. "Alright princess, let's get to the game."

The game sucked.

Not because she wasn't into baseball (although she wasn't), but because *sitting through an entire baseball game with a plug up her ass sucked.* Standing had been bad enough. Sitting was way worse. The way she clenched when the whole park screamed "O!" during the national anthem didn't help. And as she shifted back and forth, trying to find a semi-comfortable position, Ethan smirked at her constantly, obviously amused by her issue. The big jerk.

Thankfully none of his friends seemed to pick up on anything, though Trish did give her a few curious looks. After that, Ria tried to stay as still as possible.

Did it help her remember to behave? She wasn't so sure about that, but it sure distracted her from doing... anything, much less misbehaving. Just keeping up with the conversation was difficult, because she was so focused on her butt and what was up it.

It didn't help that it also turned her on. No matter how engaging the conversation, no matter how exciting a moment of the game was, she could hardly forget about Ethan and sex when she had the plug in her. Coming to her feet meant clenching around it. Sitting back down meant more squirming.

Pressing her thighs together against the waves of need constantly washing through her did very little to help.

By the time they got home, she didn't need any foreplay. *She* jumped *him*, the second they got out of the car. They barely made it inside before he fucked her, just like he'd said he would, with the plug still inside her... though she wasn't sure he'd planned to do it up against the wall like that.

Research.

CHAPTER 15

"Oh, thank goodness you finally answered, I feel like I keep missing you!" Molly whined as soon as Ria answered the phone. A wave of guilt went through her. She'd been pretty good about texting her bestie, but they hadn't actually talked on the phone once since Ria had slept with Ethan.

It felt too weird. She wasn't used to keeping secrets from Molly and it was easier when she didn't actually have to watch what she said... texting was simpler.

"I'm sorry... I've just been really busy."

"Lots of research?" Molly asked teasingly.

Heat suffused Ria's cheeks, and she was really glad this wasn't a video call, because there was no way she should be blushing like this at such a simple question.

"Um, yup. So much research." To distract herself—and her friend—from her discomfort (because of course her mind went to the extra research she'd been doing that had nothing to do with the state), she told Molly the story of her first drive across the Bay Bridge.

Molly, unsurprisingly, laughed her ass off. "You know you can literally hire someone to drive you across, right?"

"No, I did not know that." Ria sighed. "If I'd just woken up your brother it wouldn't have been a problem, but I figured I'd let him sleep."

"Mmm. Yeah, so that was really nice of him to go to the beach with you for a whole weekend." Molly's bland tone tripped an alarm in Ria's head, but she wasn't sure where the danger lay.

"It was. He's really nice."

"Oh. My. God. You slept with my brother!" Molly shrieked, and Ria's heart kicked into overdrive.

"No I didn't!" She blurted the words out in a panic, gripping the phone tightly and looking around as if Ethan might catch her spilling their secret—even though she totally hadn't and even though he was tucked away safely in his office right now. Crap!

"You so did. No one in the history of the world has called my brother 'nice' unless they were sleeping with him."

"I... well..." Ria sputtered.

"Ha!" Molly crowed. "I knew you two would be perfect together!"

"What?" Talk about emotional whiplash. That was the last thing she'd expected Molly to say, even though she hadn't seemed upset when she'd guessed Ria was sleeping with her brother. The idea that Molly had deliberately set them up, without warning her, was not on her bingo card.

"You and Ethan." It didn't matter that Ria couldn't see her bestie; she knew Molly was grinning smugly. "I knew you two would get along, and I was pretty sure you'd be into each other. There was no guarantee of course, but I had a *feeling*." She put particular emphasis on the last word.

Molly was infamous for her 'feelings' when it came to couples, but Ria had never been on the receiving end before. Which maybe should have told her something about her exes, but truthfully, she'd never really believed.

Which meant it would be silly to start now.

"We're not a couple," she said firmly. "We're just doing... research."

"Oh, reeeeesearch," Molly sang out mockingly.

"Yes, research. Because he's a Daddy Dom."

Immediately Molly started gagging. "Ew, ew, I don't want details! That's my brother!"

Well, at least Ria had that card to keep in her back pocket if Molly got annoying about Ethan and Ria hooking up. She could just start talking about his huge dick and how well he used it and Molly would probably hang up the phone.

"Okay, well just know that I'm only using him for his knowledge and his dick," Ria said primly.

"Sure you are, Miss Doesn't Sleep With a Guy Till the Fifth Date. You are definitely the type for casual sex. I totally believe you feel absolutely nothing for my brother but are having sex with him anyway."

Ria opened her mouth to say that of course she didn't feel anything romantic for Ethan and then... she couldn't make the words come out. Because they weren't true. Molly had a point, but Ria hadn't waited till a fifth date with Ethan. They hadn't even really been on a date-date, although they'd eaten plenty of meals together at this point, and yet she'd had sex with him on every reasonably comfortable flat surface in this house outside of Molly's room.

It was supposed to just be research, but she hadn't been sleeping in Molly's room. She'd been sleeping in his. In his arms. And spending all her free time with him outside of work.

"I... I'm going home soon," she said hollowly. She'd been avoiding thinking about that, because she didn't *want* to go home. She didn't want to leave Ethan.

But it wasn't like she could stay here for him. She'd just met the guy. She had a whole life back in New York. This upcoming weekend was her last one here and they were going camping, which she was excited about but... that was it. After that it was basically over.

"There's always long-distance," Molly said cheerfully. "Or you could just stay in Maryland, you know. You can write anywhere. You don't have to do it up here."

"Right..." But it was way too soon to be making life-changing decisions like that. She hadn't even known Ethan for a full month. Sure, they'd been living together that whole time, and spending all their time together, but that didn't mean they'd be able to keep on like that forever.

Right?

Ethan

Just know that I'm only using him for his knowledge and his dick.

The words echoed in Ethan's head as they drove along the highway, headed for Cunningham Falls. He was going to need to remember those words this weekend. Part of him really wished he hadn't come out of his office for a break at exactly the wrong time earlier this week, but he knew it was for the best.

He'd started thinking crazy thoughts, like, maybe he should ask Ria if she wanted to see where this thing between them went. Apparently, the universe wanted him to know that it wasn't going anywhere before his heart got any more involved. Okay, fair enough. He was concentrating on enjoying the time they had and when it was time for her to go, he'd send her off on her merry way. If her pussy was sore and his dick was chafed by the time she left, even better.

"What is that?" Ria asked, pointing out the windshield.

Ethan grinned. He hadn't warned her on purpose—not that there really was any adequate warning.

"Free Dorothy," he responded, rather than actually answering her question. He still missed seeing the graffiti on the bridge before the white castle tipped with gold that loomed out of the forest behind it.

"Oh... it does kind of look like Oz, doesn't it? I was thinking more like Sleeping Beauty's castle." Ria tilted her head, twisting a little in her seat to get a better look as they went by. "Is that... a gold statue up there?"

"Yup. When I was a kid, I thought it was Disney-land," he admitted.

"What is it actually?"

"The Mormon temple. My parents took Molly and me there to see their Christmas tree display when we were teenagers. It's pretty impressive, though also disappointing that it wasn't actually something magical."

Ria snickered. "I can see that."

She reached over, her hand creeping towards his. Ah, fuck it. Ethan let go of the steering wheel with his right hand to take her fingers in his. Might as well enjoy the moment while it was happening, and he liked holding hands with her. Next week she'd go back to New York, so rather than pouting about her leaving, he'd make the most of what time they had together.

He wasn't going to cut off his dick just to spite his face.

She looked back out the window. "I can't believe how many trees there are, right next to the highway." She shook her head.

"The state is great that way," Ethan agreed happily. "Within a couple of hours, you can go from beach, to farmland, to mountains and forest. I did a lot of hiking on the Appalachian trail when I was a kid."

"Molly told me about some of that. And something called the Goat Trail?"

"Billy Goat Trail," Ethan corrected her. "That's a good one."

"Too bad I'm heading home so soon," Ria mused. "I feel like I've barely touched the surface of the things to do around here."

"You haven't. There's also all the historical sites, especially from the Civil War, and lots of history about the Underground Railroad, plus a bunch of national parks, and a crap ton of hauntings." Ethan chuckled. "Sometime you'll have to ask Molly about her experiences at the Little Bennett Nature Center." Did he believe in ghosts? Not really, but he also wasn't foolish enough to walk into Little Bennett at night and say that out loud.

Ria nodded, still staring out the window.

Ethan gave her hand a squeeze and then released it to turn up the music on the radio. Talking about the things she was still missing out on was making his chest ache in an odd way. It made him feel dumb, but he'd gotten used to having her around. Of course he was going to miss her once she left.

That didn't mean he was heartbroken or anything. It just meant he didn't want to talk about it. They had a whole weekend to enjoy, and several days after that. She'd arrived on a Wednesday, and she was going home on a Wednesday, mostly to avoid the weekend travelers. Which made sense.

This weekend he was going to show her some hiking trails, get her out into nature, and enjoy a weekend of stargazing and cuddling in a tent. Ria seemed hesitant about it, mostly, he knew, because she'd never been camping before, but she was willing to try it out for two nights. According to her, that was how long she could be away from a real bathroom.

He'd explained that there *were* showers on site, but she seemed dubious. He supposed he couldn't blame her; it definitely weren't the same as being at home and taking a shower. It was going to be a good weekend, though he couldn't help but feel a little bittersweet about it, knowing it was the last one.

<u>Ria</u>

She was not a camping girl, it turned out.

Oh, there were things she liked about it. She did like the hiking and the campfire and the s'mores and looking up at the stars—and why did food taste better after being cooked over a campfire? But she did not like the public showers, the bugs (which were everywhere, including the showers), smelling like bug spray all day long, the constant making sure all their food and trash was secure so the animals wouldn't come calling, the lack of soft cushion when she was sleeping, and how she woke up feeling damp.

She'd much rather do the hiking and the campfire and then fall asleep and wake up in an actual bed, with an attached bathroom, where she could take a private, bug-free shower. Walking to the bathrooms to pee in the middle of the night wasn't much fun either, especially because they were so much more buggy when the bathrooms were the only lights in the area. Ethan had been great about helping chase a few creepy-crawlies out of the stall she wanted to use, but she still couldn't relax the entire time she was in there.

While hanging out in the camp chairs and doing nothing but chatting and hiking was pretty relaxing, she couldn't say it was a relaxing trip because of everything else. Somehow it was simultaneously both relaxing and stressful.

Even more so because things between her and Ethan were... off.

She couldn't define exactly what was off between them, she just knew something was. It had been the whole trip.

All she could think was that they both were struggling with knowing this was her last weekend. And she couldn't stop thinking about what Molly had said. Could they try the long-distance thing? Could she move states for a man?

Other than Molly, what *was* holding her in New York other than familiarity? Most of her friends were online.

Her parents had retired to South Carolina. She didn't have any other family in the area.

Maybe it wasn't so crazy to think of moving here. Not even just for Ethan. She'd made friends with his friends too, and she really liked all of them. The cost of living was lower. There was so much more research she could do in the state. She could literally experience multiple terrains, rather than only sticking to a city. And if she did want to keep writing about cities, she could write about the nation's capital, or Baltimore, or she could write small town or beach town or... the list of possibilities went on and on.

Though she knew the real draw was the people. Not just her new friends, but Ethan. Because she could always travel for research. Yup, she was that pathetic girl thinking about moving for a man.

Okay, but if I was ever going to consider moving for a man...

She watched him chopping up some more wood for the fire, which was basically lady porn. Not only was he deft with the hatchet, he split the wood easily with one blow, every time.

Competency kink, that's what that was.

"So... I'm going home on Wednesday." She wasn't sure how to bring up the idea of 'hey, your sister was trying to set us up, and it worked and I'm falling for you and I want to know if you're falling for me too' but she figured she'd start with the obvious fact that she was leaving. It seemed like a way to ease into the conversation and then she could segue to 'want to try long-distance?'

"I remember." He flashed a grin at her before bending over to pick up all the wood he'd just split. "Oh, hey,

Caitlyn and Trish were wondering if you'd want to do a little goodbye party thing on Tuesday."

"Oh... yeah, I would like that." Part of her had been thinking that was her last night with Ethan and they'd fuck and cuddle, but she did also want to see the others...

"Great. They're really going to miss you." He flashed her another grin and her heart ached a little bit. What about him, was he going to miss her too?

Ask, dumbass. In a flirty way, not a pathetic way.

"Are you going to miss me too?" Okay that sounded decently flirty with just a tinge of desperation that he hopefully wouldn't notice.

Ethan chuckled. With the way he was crouched in front of the fire, she couldn't really see his expression very clearly, which was frustrating. She squirmed in her seat, feeling antsy. "Well, my dick definitely will," he joked, and Ria managed to push a smile on her face.

That definitely hadn't been what she meant. And it didn't really feel like an 'Ethan' answer. Maybe that was just how he dealt with the idea of missing her? "I'm going to miss you."

Finally, he looked up at her, his expression more serious. "I'll miss you too. You're always welcome to come visit. I'm sure Molly will insist on it."

Okay, this was good, she could work with this.

"Do you think you'd ever come up to New York to visit?" she asked.

Ethan snorted. "Absolutely fucking not. I hate New York. There's a reason I've never come to visit Molly."

"Oh..." She wished she was brave enough to ask if he'd come visit for *her*, but if he wasn't willing to visit for his sister... plus, the first thing he'd said was no. Not just no either, but 'fuck' no.

So that was that. She was leaving on Wednesday. He was never going to come to New York, not even for her. Which made sense since they'd only been spending time together for a few weeks. Who jumped into a long-distance relationship after that?

Wasn't going to be her and Ethan, apparently.

CHAPTER 16

<u>RIA</u>

The last morning. Ria's heart ached. As did her pussy. After the goodbye party last night, Ethan had kept her up for half the night... and then she'd fallen asleep in his arms while he held her, trying not to cry because it was for the last time.

"So um... I guess I'll see you if I visit with Molly again."

"Or if you ever need to do more research." Ethan's smile didn't reach his eyes, which were sad.

"Or if you visit New York," she countered, in one last desperate attempt to see if that was a possibility.

Ethan laughed like she was joking.

She smiled, to pretend his laughter didn't make her heart hurt.

It wasn't his fault he didn't feel the same way she did, and she wasn't going to mar their goodbye by being *that girl*. They'd had a good time of it, and they were going to end on a good note, even though she was feeling far more heartbroken than she had any right to.

"Right, if I ever visit New York," he said, still joking, and this time his eyes actually had a little sparkle in them, which killed the slim measure of hope she'd been holding. He really couldn't even consider the notion except as a joke, even when she was leaving, which meant this really was completely over. Stepping forward, Ethan wrapped her in a big hug, and she squeezed him back, happy to be able to hide her face against his broad chest. "Take care of yourself, princess."

"You too." She managed to cut herself off before she called him Daddy. Even though he'd just called her princess, it didn't seem appropriate. He wasn't going to be *her* Daddy Dom anymore.

He was a Maryland Daddy, not a New York one.

Taking a deep breath, she gathered herself and pulled away. "I need to get going or I'm going to be on the road forever." She pushed another smile onto her face. Ethan smiled back and stepped away, letting his arms drop. She didn't think she was fooling herself that he was having as much trouble saying goodbye as she was, but that didn't mean things would work out if they tried to extend them.

It was better to leave it like this, end their research agreement right when they said they would, before their emotions got more involved.

Ria got into her car and gave him another wave before backing out of the driveway. Ethan stood there watching her. After waving back to her, he shoved his hands in his pockets, his smile completely gone from his face. She waved again and started off down the road, refusing to look back.

It should have gotten easier. She should have felt lighter as she went, now that the tension had been broken.

Her chest should loosen, she should be able to take deeper breaths...

Instead, her chest felt like it was getting tighter and tighter as she drove down the street and turned the corner. Her eyes burned as her air constricted, a tight band squeezing her painfully, and Ria pulled off to the side of the road. Thankfully she was still in Ethan's neighborhood, though no longer visible to his street.

Pressing her hands to her chest, she couldn't hold back the sob that ripped out of her.

Because he had been perfect. He'd been her first Daddy. The first man that actually met all of her needs and more. And she was driving away from him... because he didn't want her the same way she wanted him. And it fucking hurt so bad.

Five minutes. She gave herself five minutes to sob her heart out before she caught her composure and started taking long, deep breaths in as she counted to five, and then let it back out. She blew her nose and wiped her tears away. Took another deep breath and straightened up in her seat.

It was time to go home.

Back to her lonely apartment in New York City where she could have a tub of ice cream delivered and eat the entire thing in the privacy of her own home while crying over her stupidly broken heart. She'd found one amazing Daddy Dom; she could find another one. They were out there. Ethan had been the first, he didn't have to be the last.

Ethan

The house was lonely without Ria. It took less than a day for him to realize it and more than a week for him to admit it. Part of that was because he'd started reading her books after she left.

All of them.

So, he was at least a little distracted from having to admit how much he missed her as the days, and then weeks, rolled by. Reading her books made him feel a tiny bit closer to her. But every time he finished a book, he couldn't stop thinking about her, so he'd pick another one up. It was a double-edged sword.

"Earth to Ethan, come in Ethan." Trish waved her hand in front of his face and Ethan jerked back. "Welcome back to the party, bro. Did you even hear the question?"

"No," he admitted. Ever since Ria had left for New York, he hadn't been very helpful at trivia. Or at socializing in general. The biggest mistake had definitely been letting her hang out with his friends so much. He hadn't been able to do anything about Molly letting Ria use her room, so his home was full of memories, but now he couldn't even spend time with his friends.

He knew that she and the girls had a group chat.

He knew that her last book set in New York was finished and with her editor.

He knew she had started working on her new series that was set in Maryland.

He knew she'd been asking the girls a bunch of questions about Maryland.

And he knew she did not have any current plans to come back to visit.

None of the information he had made him feel better.

He should have kept his dick in his pants. Except he

couldn't really wish for that because he didn't really regret the time he'd spent with her... He just regretted letting her go.

Maybe if he'd had just a little *more* time with her, he could have shown her how good they would be together. Made her want to stay with him.

"Ethan!"

"What?" he snapped, and then clenched his jaw because he was aware of his friends all exchanging glances. Yes, he knew he was being a crabby dick lately, but it would help if everyone wasn't constantly riding his ass. Thankfully, his phone started buzzing before anyone could chide him. He pulled it out of his pocket and held it up. "It's Molly, I've got to take this."

He got to his feet, ignoring the glances that were being shot around the table, and headed to the door. It was too loud in the bar to hear her, though he did answer it, so she didn't get sent to voicemail.

"Hey Moll, give me a second, I'm at the bar and I'm heading outside." If she responded he couldn't hear it. Walking through the door to the exterior was night and day when it came to the sound. Quiet reined outside, despite the people on the patio, because all the conversation spread out and dissipated into the open air. Ethan pressed the phone to his ear. "Okay, what's up?"

"You tell me. Caitlyn says you're being a dick."

Closing his eyes, Ethan pinched the bridge of his nose.

"Are you seriously calling me because my ex told you I'm being a dick?" Maybe he'd been better off back inside with his friends. At least they'd be partly distracted by the trivia.

"I'm calling you because every single one of your

friends has texted me that you're being a dick over the past couple weeks, and Caitlyn texted me to tell me that you're being a dick *right now*, and I'm tired of hearing about what an asshat you're being." Molly didn't pause for breath as she harangued him, stirring up plenty of guilt as he inwardly acknowledged the truth of her words, but then she said something he hadn't been expecting. "I'm tired of you being a dick and obviously bent out of shape while Ria's up here crying into her ice cream, all because you two idiots couldn't even *try* to make a long-distance relationship work."

"What long-distance relationship?" he asked indignantly, though his brain immediately caught onto the 'crying into her ice cream' thing. He dismissed it just as quickly. Molly had to be exaggerating. Ria had been perfectly fine when she'd left. "Hell, what relationship? She was just using my dick for research."

Crap. The moment he said the words he knew they were a mistake, because he would never have said it like that to Molly... no, he'd gotten that exact phrasing direct from Ria. That those words were still bothering him was revealing in a manner that he hadn't intended to share.

"You heard Ria telling me that." It wasn't a question. Molly was mulling over this new information.

Ethan sighed. "It's fine, Molly, you're just seeing things that aren't there."

"No, I had a feeling about you two, that's part of why I sent her down there."

Ethan groaned. "You had a feeling about Pierce and Trish too, and look at how that's going."

"They'll get there," Molly replied stubbornly. "But that's not the point. The point is, you're being a miserable asshole ever since Ria came back to New York, and she's been crying into her ice cream and pretending she's doing no such thing. You overheard one thing she said and decided that was the entirety of a complicated situation."

That was the second time Molly had said Ria was crying into her ice cream in less than five minutes.

"Why would she be crying?" he asked irritably. "She's the one who chose to go back home."

"Seriously, that's what you got out of everything I just said?" Molly made an exasperated noise. "Yes, Ria's acting like she just went through a major breakup. You're acting like you just went through a major breakup. But you didn't need to break up! Why on earth would you tell her that you'd never visit her in New York?"

"She didn't ask me to!"

Something in his brain pinged though. No, she hadn't asked him to come visit her... but she had asked if he'd ever come visit. He thought she'd meant generally. He'd answered in the way he always had, especially after Molly had moved there and had been bugging him to visit *her*.

He hadn't taken it as Ria asking if he'd come visit her if they were in a relationship.

Which... okay, no, he wouldn't really *want* to, but he *would* do it.

Molly was ranting at him though and he hadn't been paying attention.

"You guys didn't even talk. Do you know how frustrating it is to watch two people *not* communicate? And, like why? It's so easy. You say, 'I like you' and then she says 'I like you, too' and then you figure out how to keep things going... or let her know that you don't want her to leave."

"Hey, she could have done the same," he protested,

but deep down he already knew it was different. Even if Ria wasn't submissive, even if he wasn't the Daddy Dom, asking to stay in someone's house with them was very different than asking someone to stay. And she had asked him if he'd come to New York, even if his brain hadn't parsed out what she was *actually* asking at the time.

Fuck.

He'd fucked up.

But if she was still crying into her ice cream that meant he had a chance to fix it, right? She wouldn't be crying at all if she didn't feel the same way he did, if she was truly past the time they'd spent together and wanted to move on from it.

There was only one thing he could do. And he hated to do it, but sometimes sacrifices had to be made for the greater good.

"Molly, I'm going to need your help."

CHAPTER 17

A baseball game. Of all the places Molly could have dragged her to. Though, at least this time she didn't have a plug up her ass.

And was she such a sad sack that part of her felt a little weepy about not having a plug up her ass?

Yes. Yes, she was.

Pathetic.

But getting out into public and doing something with a friend was part of getting over a breakup. Even if it hadn't really been a breakup because they hadn't really been in a relationship.

Which was why, when Molly scored free tickets from a co-worker and begged Ria to go with her, Ria said yes. Which meant that going to a baseball game should be no big deal. If only she could stop thinking about Ethan for even one second of it, it wouldn't be.

A roar went up from the crowd, and Ria made a face when she looked up and saw the Kiss Cam on the screens above the stands. Normally she liked the Kiss Cam, but right now it felt like everyone was rubbing their happy couple-ness in her face, kicking her while she was down. She knew it wasn't personal, but it still made her feel grumpy.

Next to her, Molly brushed off her lap and leaned forward, glancing back at Ria. "I'm gonna go get another beer, you want anything?" Molly asked as she got to her feet.

"Sure, thanks," Ria said, pushing a smile on her face. It wasn't Molly's fault Ria was in a foul mood. Ria wasn't sure that Molly even knew she'd even been to a game with Ethan, or what that game had meant to her. Plus, she'd been doing what she could to shield her pathetic reaction to coming home from her bestie, so that hopefully Molly wouldn't realize how invested she'd gotten in their non-relationship.

Taking a deep breath, she looked up at the screen to watch the Kiss Cam. This could be like desensitization. Because it wasn't like she could avoid couples until her heart stopped hurting so much. And it seemed to be working, because after the first two, she started smiling again.

Love was out there. One day she would find what she was looking for. She truly did believe that, and seeing the couples being caught by the Kiss Cam gave her a little boost of hope.

Movement out of the corner of her eye let her know Molly was back, the thud of Molly's body hitting the seat much louder than Ria expected—somehow her brain knew before she even turned to see her friend that it was *not* Molly beside her. As she turned, she caught a glimpse of *herself* on the Kiss Cam.

Herself and the man who had taken his sister's seat. Shock parted her lips as her expected reality twisted, changing so abruptly that everything suddenly felt completely surreal.

Ethan caught her face in his hands and pulled her in, catching her lips with his. The crowd roared as Ria kissed him back, the feel of him touching her, kissing her, was grounding in a way she would have never expected.

He's here! He's really here!

Which was exactly what she said when he finally pulled away, her face still cradled in his hands.

"You're here." She blinked in shock. Here and wearing a Baltimore Orioles shirt, which was what let her know it was really him. "You're in New York. You don't come to New York." It was the only thing she could think of to say.

"I came for you."

Her heart did a flip as he leaned in to kiss her again. There was no roar of the crowd, but there were a few catcalls around them as he did so.

He's here! What is he doing here? He's here for ME. *He said that!*

What does it mean?

It means he loves you and you're going to live happily ever after!

No, that was just her brain on romance. That didn't happen in real life.

But he came to New York. For me. He doesn't even come here for his sister.

Ethan pulled away again so he could look into her eyes. "I'm sorry I let you leave Maryland without telling you what you mean to me. I didn't realize you wanted anything more than... research, and I overheard a conversation you were having with Molly that backed that up."

"Oh no," Ria whispered. "I'm sorry. I didn't... I was trying to convince myself of something that wasn't true."

"I think I understand that now." He gave her a rueful smile. "We have some work to do on communication and I want to start right here and now. Ria, I was falling in love with you before you left Maryland. I have missed the fuck out of you since you've been gone. I want to try to make a relationship with you work, even if I have to come up to New York every weekend for the next year."

"What if I asked you to move here?" she teased, but he winced anyway, even though her tone was clearly joking, which made her laugh.

"If we got to that point, I would seriously consider it. For you."

It wasn't a yes, but it was a huge concession coming from him and she knew it.

The truth was, she wasn't that attached to staying in New York anyway. She'd been missing the fuck out of him too, but she'd also been missing Maryland. She hated having to ask so many questions of the people she'd left behind, rather than being able to go experience the answers for herself. She'd missed him, his friends, the beach, the trees... everything. Which was why she needed to admit the truth.

"I'd rather move to Maryland, if it comes to that," she admitted with a smile. "I was already planning to come back for a long-term rental soon. I've been looking at places online."

Ethan closed his eyes and sighed before opening them again and giving her a *look*. "Does Molly know about this?" he asked.

"Of course." Ria grinned as he shook his head and muttered something unintelligible under his breath. Her bestie was apparently plotting on multiple ends. "Though, I'll admit, my plan was to avoid you at first. Maybe for a while."

"Well, good luck with that now that you're my girlfriend."

"Oh I am?" Ria couldn't help but sass back, even as a thrill went through her at his statement. "You aren't going to ask me or anything?"

"Nah." He sat back in the seat, his arm slung around the back of hers, his hand curving over her shoulder. Then he leaned over, his fingers trailing up to her neck, where they rested gently but with the threat of something more, and Ria's breath caught in her throat. "Because you're a good girl, and goods girls do what Daddy tells them to."

Well, there went her panties.

Ethan

Giving himself an erection in the middle of a baseball game had *not* been the plan. On the other hand, maybe he should have expected it. After his time with Ria, she was the bell, and his dick was the dog. Thanks Pavlov. Just the image he needed in his head.

But it was true.

He made himself sit through the whole game with her though, rather than carrying her off over his shoulder the way he wanted to, because the more important thing was that she knew he wasn't here just for the sex. That was a bonus, of course, but he was here for her. Even though he wasn't normally a grand gesture type of guy, he'd wanted to make it, to show her he cared and was committed to making a long-distance relationship work if she was.

Going by her reaction to his appearance, she was on the same page.

And even with an erection, it was nice just to spend time with her again. He did glance over his shoulder a few times to make sure Molly was doing well in her seat, which was quite a few rows back. Ethan had gotten a good spot where he'd been able to keep an eye on Ria the whole time, waiting for the right moment to come down... the Kiss Cam had been the signal.

One of Molly's friends ran the camera feed for it and had been easily bribed with some Broadway tickets to span over to Ria's seat once Ethan was there.

There had been a lot of moving parts, but it came together beautifully and was more than worth it to be by her side again.

He even got her some popcorn to eat, sending her into gales of laughter when he pulled out his keychain with the tiny Old Bay cannister on it to spice up the bucket. Hey, he came prepared.

"So how does this compare to an Orioles game?" he asked, during a lull in the action.

Ria rolled her eyes, giving him an exasperated look. "You know they're really all about the same, right?"

Ethan put his hand over his heart, pretending to be mortally wounded and shaking his head in denial, which made her laugh. He grinned back at her, enjoying the banter.

Eventually they were finally able to file out of the park and head back to her place. Molly had offered him her couch in case things went horribly wrong, but he wasn't going to need it. Instead, he got to see how Ria lived.

Her studio apartment was small but cozy, with over-stuffed bookshelves lining every open space on the wall. Ethan could only shake his head. She clearly needed more space for more bookshelves. Maybe a whole library. He didn't get much of a chance to peruse any titles though, because as soon as she had the door closed and locked behind them, she threw herself into his arms.

Which was exactly where he wanted her.

Damn but she felt good back where she belonged.

Ethan claimed her lips with his own, kissing her with the hunger that had been building for weeks. Moaning against his lips, Ria rubbed herself against him like a cat in heat, just as eager for him as he was for her. He ran his hands over her body, feeling her squirm against his erect cock, as he got them headed for her bed.

"Fuck I missed you," he murmured as he pulled his lips away so he could tug her shirt off over her head.

"I missed you too," she said, returning the favor before running her hands down his bare chest until she reached his belt.

"I love you." Saying the words out loud made both of them pause, but he didn't want to take them back. He meant them. Losing her had made him realize exactly how much his emotions had gotten engaged.

"I love you too." She breathed out the words and then their clothes were falling from them in record time, they were so eager to get their hands on each other.

But Ethan had a very specific plan.

He'd read all her books by now, and he'd come to New York knowing exactly what he wanted to do with

Ria once he got there. He was going to claim her once and for all.

Sitting down on the edge of the bed, he pulled her toward him so he could start stripping off her capris.

"You've been very naughty, princess," he said with a grin as he undid the button and started to peel the fabric down her legs. "Coming back to New York and not calling me."

"Oh, I'm so sorry, Daddy... I didn't know I was supposed to be the one to call you," she sassed back at him, making him chuckle.

His dick throbbed at hearing her call him 'Daddy' again. "That's okay, princess, you're going to make it up to me." Now that she was stripped down, he pulled her over his lap, naked butt up in the air. "First I'm going to spank this naughty bottom, and then Daddy's going to fuck it."

"What?" Ria squealed, bucking on his lap, her hands coming up to cover her butt—as if that would help. Ethan took both wrists in one hand and pinned them down in the middle of her back—which also pinned her against his legs.

"You heard me, princess," he said, running his hand over the smooth, pale curve of her ass. "Unless you say your safe word, Daddy's going to spank your naughty bottom and then he's going to fuck it."

Going by her books, that was one of Ria's deepest fantasies—and butt stuff meant 'I love you.'

"Daddy noooooo," she moaned, squirming against his leg. He could feel the heat coming off her pussy, and when his fingers brushed against the swollen lips, he could feel how wet she was.

"That's not your safe word, princess," he answered

with a smirk. Then he raised his hand and brought it down hard on her upturned bottom, eliciting a delightful shriek from her.

Damn but he'd missed making her squeal like that.

CHAPTER 18

RIA

Daddy's going to fuck my naughty bottom.

The thought was terrifying and thrilling at the same time. She'd wanted Ethan to be the one to take that particular cherry when she'd been in Maryland, but she never voiced it because... well... it seemed so horribly intimate. Not something to do with someone she had no future with.

She wanted to save that for someone special.

The fact that it *was* Ethan and that he was talking like a hero straight out of her books had her swooning. Being reminded that 'no' wasn't her safe word made her pussy clench.

There was no way she was saying 'meatloaf' or 'red' now though.

Nope. She wanted this. All of it.

Even the spanking, which made her butt sting with every slap of his palm against her flesh.

"Daddy, please, I'll be a good girl!" she squealed as his hand came down again, hard enough to make her legs kick, hard enough to heat her insides, hard enough that she lifted her bottom in the air for more.

"That's right... you're going to be my good girl from now on, aren't you?" He spanked her again and Ria bucked, moaning as the heat flared through her.

She could feel Daddy's erection digging into her side, rubbing against her as she squirmed on his lap. "Yes, Daddy, I promise."

All the promise got her was face down on the bed, pink butt high in the air, with Daddy's fingers pushing into her bottom and stretching her open. Ria moaned at the sensation, burying her face in her pillow as her insides quivered. He'd freaking brought the lube with him.

For one short moment, she'd remembered that *she* didn't have any lube and felt the oddest mixture of relief and disappointment, before Daddy proved what a Boy Scout he was. Always be prepared... for anal sex. His fingers opened inside her, making her pant as he added a third one to the mix, stretching her even more, and Ria whimpered.

This was different from the plug, not in the least because his fingers were moving and twisting and setting off all sorts of little pleasure nerve endings. There was no nook for her ring to settle into, instead it was being stretched over and over again as his knuckles passed through, but without being able to get anywhere near to fully closed in between.

"Daddy it's too much," she whined, as his three fingers moved inside her, stroking her and leaving her pussy aching emptily.

"You can take it, princess," he crooned, and it might have been her imagination, but it felt like he thrust his fingers in even harder. "You're going to be taking some-thing bigger in just a moment."

Ria shuddered, her hole clenching around him, trying to hold him in place, but it was impossible with the lube.

Bigger.

She craved it even as she feared it.

And when his fingers slipped out of her, for the brief moments it took him to wipe them off on the damp cloth he had prepared, and lube up his cock, all Ria could do was quiver in tensely excited anticipation.

"Daddy!" She gasped as she felt him press against her entrance. It opened easily enough, after all the stretching his fingers had done, but it felt entirely different than his fingers had.

Softer. Blunter. Thicker.

Ethan groaned as he gripped her hips, holding her in place while his cock began to slide deeper into her bowels. She cried out at the sensation... it really was bigger than his fingers, and she could feel every centimeter as his cock slowly impaled her.

"Oh God..." She felt him bottom out, his body coming to rest against her cheeks, her tight hole clenching around the base of his cock, muscles working to try and push out the invader.

"He can't help you now," Ethan replied. Another time the response might have made her laugh, but all she could do was cry out as he began to retreat, the odd sensation of the huge cock pulling away like wave receding inside her. It didn't hurt, but it didn't feel good either, and yet the discomfort turned her on even more.

Knowing that she was doing this for him, that she was taking the sting, the burn of being stretched open so widely, the discomfort of having him in her most forbidden hole, was making her pussy drip with arousal.

"Daddy please!"

"You're doing great, princess, taking Daddy's cock up your sweet little ass. Your little hole looks so pretty stretched around my cock." His fingers dug into her flesh, squeezing and kneading as he began the long slide back in. "I want you to come for me while Daddy's cock is in your ass."

His words curled around her, stoking the fire that was already raging, and Ria's elbows buckled. With Daddy gripping her hips so tightly, that meant the rest of her wasn't going anywhere, leaving her ass high in the air while her upper body rested against the bed. Her breasts swayed beneath her, nipples rubbing against her comforter, stimulating her even more.

Daddy moved one hand away from her hip and then Ria heard a buzzing noise that didn't entirely register until that same hand moved beneath her, pressing a small vibrator against her clit just as he began to thrust. Ria chocked on a scream at the assault of sensations, the sting and discomfort mingling with the buzzing pleasure from the toy Daddy was rubbing her clit with. It was too much and yet exactly right all at the same time.

"That's it, princess, come for Daddy." He pressed the vibrator more firmly against her and Ria screamed into the pillow as she came while Daddy fucked her ass.

Ethan

The vibrator had been necessary because Ethan wanted Ria to enjoy her first time with anal, and he knew he wasn't going to be able to last long. The way she clenched around him, her inner muscles massaging the length of his cock as he buried himself in her ass over and over again was enough to drive him wild. He held the vibrator against her clit as she bucked beneath him, sobbing out her climax.

His own peak slammed into him, and he groaned as he impaled her fully, forcing himself into her clenching hole all the way to the hilt.

"Fuck!"

Her rippling muscles milked his cock, spurt after spurt emptying into her bowels, filling her with his release. Ethan pulled the vibrator away as she went limp beneath him, sliding down onto the bed with him atop her, his cock still lodged in her ass as they came to rest.

Flicking the vibrator off, he rolled, pulling her with him, so they were in the classic spooning position. Even as his cock softened, it was reluctant to leave the warm haven of her body. With his arms wrapped around her, his hands full of her breasts, his leg tossed over hers, he didn't think they could get much closer... and it was everything he wanted. Everything he'd been missing.

"So... you're thinking of moving to Maryland, huh?" he murmured against the back of her neck. Fingers lightly stroked over his arms and he felt, more than heard, her small laugh. His cock finally slipped from her body and he sighed at the loss, but at least he could still be curled up around her.

"Yes. Though, now that I know you'd be happy to have me there, I've moved from thinking about it to definitely doing it."

"Mm. Need a place to stay?"

This time he could hear her delighted laugh.

"Moving kind of fast, aren't you?"

Ethan shrugged, shifting so he could roll her onto her back and look down at her, his head propped up on one of his hands.

"When I know I want something, I go and get it. Please see Exhibit A." He grinned waving his hand over her body before leaning down for a kiss. Ria's hands came up to slide across his jawline before hooking behind his neck as she kissed him back.

"You came to New York for me." She grinned up at him as she broke the kiss.

"That's right. You and only you. You can ask Molly; I haven't been to visit her once since she moved here."

Ria shook her head. "You know that even with me coming to Maryland, that's going to have to change. I'm still going to want to visit here, and I won't want to do it alone."

"Mmm... I'm sure you'll be able to find a way to make it up to me." He ran his hand down her body, curving his fingers around her hip and making her laugh again. "Especially if you move in with me."

Ria eyed him speculatively, pressing her lips together. "I'll think about it."

EPILOGUE

One Month Later

RIA

"I can't believe you're kicking me out of your house for your girlfriend," Molly complained.

"You're not being kicked out; you're just having to move your stuff that you haven't even been using to the basement—which is what you offered to do for her!" Ethan was getting exasperated with his sister, exactly as she intended, which had Ria cracking up. He was seemingly incapable of not letting Molly get under his skin right now.

Molly had offered to let Ria have her room as an office now that she was moving in with Ethan, but she just had to give Ethan a hard time about it.

"My childhood room... gone..." Molly said with a fake sob, putting the back of her hand up to her forehead, as Pierce and Ethan carried her mattress out of the room.

"Molly, you're going to give Ethan an aneurysm," Ria said, sidling up to her friend's side. "If you really want us to leave the room intact, we can."

"No, you need an office." Molly sighed, putting her hands on her hips and looking around. "It's just weird. I had this idea in my head that this room would always be here for me, but life moves on. It's probably better this way. Extra motivation to make things work for me in New York."

"Hey, if it doesn't, you can always come back here. We *will* make room for you," Ria said firmly, secure in the knowledge that Ethan would back her up one hundred percent. It might make certain things awkward, because they were pretty used to having sex whenever and wherever the desire struck, but they could adjust.

"Thanks." Molly reached out and gave Ria a huge hug. "I am not planning on needing it though. This house is my past, but it's your and Ethan's future."

"Well... we'll see." Ria blushed furiously. Yeah, obviously she wanted a future with Ethan, or she wouldn't be moving in with him, especially so quickly, but... somehow it felt weird to say it out loud.

"Oh no," Molly said, pulling away and glaring at her. "None of this hedging your bets stuff or thinking that just because something good is happening to you that admitting it can ruin it. Say it out loud. This house is your and Ethan's future."

Well, crap. Though, Ria had to admit, all the times Molly had made her do this, she'd been right.

"This house is mine and Ethan's future." The words rang oddly in the air, but at the same time, something settled in her heart. If saying things out loud could make them true, that one felt like it had landed.

This house was her and Ethan's future. Because she found her Daddy Dom, the man she loved, the man she wanted to spend the rest of her life with. And no, it wasn't too soon to say that, dammit.

The heart didn't always operate on a logical schedule.

"Come on," she said, giving Molly one last little squeeze. "Let's get your shit out of my office."

Molly cracked up and they were both laughing as they started ferrying boxes downstairs, leaving the heaviest stuff to the guys. Between the four of them, it didn't take them long to have the bedroom turned into an office... and then Pierce and Molly left, and it was just Ethan and Ria.

"Finally," he said, taking her by the hand and pulling her back into the house from where they'd been waving goodbye to his sister and Pierce. "I've been waiting for this moment."

"Me too?" But it came out as a question because she wasn't exactly sure what he was referring to, especially since he seemed to have a mission as he pulled her along through the house. There was something specific in mind that he was heading for, and it took her a moment to realize it was Molly's old room slash her new office.

"This is the only room we haven't christened, but now that it's your office, we're claiming it as ours."

Ria had to laugh. "So, we're claiming it as ours by sticking your penis in it like a flagpole?"

Ethan gave her bottom a sharp whack, sending her though the door ahead of him and making her squeal. "No, we're claiming it by me putting my penis in you while we're in this room." He maneuvered her toward her desk, which was almost completely empty except for her computer. She knew it wasn't going to stay that way for long though. By tomorrow evening she'd have papers and things scattered all over it.

If she was going to be bent over it and fucked, this was definitely the day.

"You're ridiculous," she replied, laughing as she wound her arms around his neck. Ethan took her by the hips and lifted her up onto the desk, letting her legs hang down while he stepped between her knees.

He wasn't smiling, but his eyes were flashing with heat as he came closer, the corners of his lips tipped up just a bit.

"No, I'm Daddy." Gripping her ponytail, he pulled her hair back to tilt her lips up toward his for a kiss. Hot need rolled through her, unfurling like a wave through her core.

She was his princess, and he was her Maryland Daddy.

THE END

ABOUT GOLDEN ANGEL

Golden Angel is a *USA Today* best-selling author of heart and bottom warming romance.

She is happily married, old enough to know better but still too young to care, and a big fan of happily-ever-afters, strong heroes and heroines, and sizzling chemistry.

When she's not writing, she can often be found on the couch reading, in front of her sewing machine making a new cosplay, hanging out with her friends, or wandering the Maryland Renaissance Fair.

Daddies Everywhere

Chef Daddy

Taco Daddy

Cheese Daddy

Foosball Daddies

Zodiac Masters

Leo

Dad Bod Doms

Logan

Rawhide Ranch

A Mischievous Little Mardi Gras

A Little Double Wedding

Black Light

Defended

Black Light Roulette: War

Black Light Roulette: Finale

Dirty Heroes Collection

The Lady

Masters of Marquis

Bondage Buddies

Master Chef

Law and Disorder

Switch Play

Legally Bound

Shallow Submission

Hidden Away

Secret Submission

Third Wheel

Dungeons & Doms

Dungeon Master

Dungeon Daddy

Dungeon Showdown

Venus Rising Series

The Venus School

Venus Aspiring

Venus Desiring

Venus Transcendent

Venus Wedding